The Runaway

The Runaway

by

Patricia M. St. John

MOODY PRESS
CHICAGO

1

It is difficult to say when, exactly, this story started because, like the flowers, we are born with a longing to grow toward the light. But I think I first became conscious of that longing on a fair summer morning when I lounged on a stretch of beach to the north of Tyre and hated my sister and hated myself for hating her because, after all, it was not her fault that she was ill; or, as people in the village whispered, possessed of a devil.

I did not hate her because of the violent fits of rage that would suddenly seize her, when she would clench her teeth, tear her hair, and throw herself on to the floor or into the fire or wherever she happened to be standing. This had been going on, at intervals, for years and I had got used to it. Besides, between whiles, she sometimes seemed quite normal, although always a little strange and withdrawn. She would sit with her hands clasped, staring into space, with that old, unchildlike expression on her face, and sometimes, when she spoke, her voice sounded as though it came from a very, very long distance. But her words were often wise words, and my mother almost worshiped her.

Nobody else mattered, I thought viciously, burrowing my bare toes into the sand. I was the only son, but if the fishing catch was poor and food was scarce, it was I and my younger sister who went hungry that she might be delicately fed. There were times when I thought my mother was afraid of her, and at other times I thought that she just loved her so deeply that she was scarcely aware of anyone else. I sighed and spat and longed to be old enough to go out with my father and the net at night. But he would not take me till I was twelve, and there were yet two months to go before I attained to that age of manhood.

It was very quiet on the beach. The sun had risen over the snow-streaked crest of Mount Hermon and warmed my back, but the heat-haze still lay over sea and land so that it was impossible to tell where the sea ended and the sky began. Not a ripple broke on the sand; the water was smooth saffron melting away into bright mist and any moment now a dark speck would appear, rapidly growing bigger as it came toward me.

It was late, and that usually meant a good catch. I strained my eyes and caught sight of the boat with the net bobbing behind it and the shimmering reflection below. I ran to the edge of the water and waved, and my strong, silent father stood in the bows and waved back, and, although we did this almost every morning of my life, it was a good moment for me for I loved my father, and fishermen who went out at night did not always come back in the morning.

I ran for the baskets and was back in time to hear the grate of the keel on the sand and to feel my father's great hand as he leaped from the boat. The men were in good spirits, the boat was loaded and the net was heavy. We took our positions on the rope in silence, as a well-trained team, and I ran to the far end, a small extra, for although I was a sturdy lad, I could not have worked with the mighty brown muscles and controlled energy of the fishermen. They tensed and leaned back as one man, relaxed in split-second unity, drew one great breath all together and tensed again until the net dragged on the shore and we all ran to sort the fish.

I loved the fish; some we threw back into the water, but today they were mostly edible. We piled them into baskets, dripping, silver and shiny, heaved the baskets onto our shoulders and started for the market. But I ran back first and plunged into the sea for, although the shadows were still long, the sun was hot, and I had worked hard. Then I picked up my smaller basket and caught up with my father. The fish vendors were waiting for us in the shade of the market awning and the haggling and bargaining began. I was proud of my father, for no one could beat down his prices much, and ours was the first boat in that morning. When the price was fixed, the fish was weighed and poured out on to the slabs in great shining heaps; then my father turned to me.

"Take what is left in your basket home," he said, "and tell your mother to make ready. I will be back soon."

I started up the street that led to our home, still clad only in my fisherman's loincloth, my troubles, for the moment, forgotten. I was very hungry, and today we would eat well. My mother and little sister would gut the fish, blow up the fire, and very soon the house would be filled with the good smell of sizzling oil, of fresh fish frying, of herbs and fresh bread. My father would come and we would gather around the platter. What a good time it would be, if it were not for the haunting presence of my older sister! Usually she ate a little apart, her plate filled with the best of everything, but sometimes she would come and join us in the family circle and then we would usually fall silent, as though a stranger had joined us, and my mother would stop eating and gaze at her with that expression of yearning, frightened love, and I would stuff the rest of my meal into my mouth and run outside to get away from it all.

It was going to be a very hot day. One of the crew stood in his doorway and called to me. I stopped inside the vine-shaded porch and he gave me a drink of buttermilk while we chatted. I liked visiting the other fisher lads, but I was also ashamed; I could never ask them to my house, for I never knew when the rage and sickness would take hold of my sister. She seldom left the house by day, but everybody knew about her and whispered about her, and visitors seldom came to see us.

The buttermilk dulled the edge of my hunger, and I lingered for a time. Fish was quickly prepared, but the bread took a while to bake, and my father would not be home just yet. He had business to discuss in the market, and he liked sitting about with the other fishermen talking about the tides and the weather and the catch. Sometimes I wondered if he found it as hard as I did to come from the fresh freedom of dawn skies and the immensity of the sea, to sit under the dark shadow that lay across our home; but he was a good husband and a dutiful father, and if he shared my thoughts he had never voiced them.

I left my friend and hurried up the street for, by now, I knew that I was late. But I was still surprised, when I turned the corner, to see my mother standing in the street watching anxiously for my return. When she saw me, she ran to meet me and there was a gaiety about her that I had not seen for a long time.

"Hurry, boy," she cried impatiently. "Give me the fish. Wash and put on your tunic. Your uncle from Galilee is here, waiting for his breakfast."

I ran up the street ahead of her, for this was good news indeed. I liked my uncle from Galilee, and we had not seen him for some time. He was my mother's older brother, who had fallen in love with a girl from Capernaum. As her family had utterly refused to let her leave the land of Israel he had transferred his boat to the lake and carried on his business in Galilee. In order to placate her father, he had become a Jewish convert, but the bond between him and my mother was still close, and from time to time he came to see us.

My uncle was a big, black-bearded man with the broad physique and huge muscles of the fisherman. Seated on the mattress, resting after his long walk, he teased my delighted little sister. He also spoke courteously to my older sister but he did not joke with her, nor look much in her direction, for no one wanted to meet the gaze of those wild, intent eyes. When I spoke to her, I always looked in the other direction.

Clean and clothed, I bounded into the room and greeted my uncle joyfully. I think I was his favorite, and now he talked to me as man to man.

"Been out with the boats, boy?" he asked casually.

"Not until I'm twelve, but it won't be long now. I give a hand with the net and the catch every morning."

"Looking forward to it?"

I nodded.

He smiled. "It's in our blood, boy, from generation to generation. When my times comes to go, I hope I go down in a storm. There's something glorious about the storms on Galilee. They come down, all of a sudden, from the pockets of the hills when you're least expecting them, whipping up the water till you think your last hour has come. But I wouldn't give it up for anything; nothing like it!" The subject seemed to remind him of something for he paused, shaking his head. "Can't understand them," he continued thoughtfully. "Four of my friends have just thrown up their boats and gone on a wild goose chase; ah! here comes your father, and I can smell the fish frying."

He leaped to his feet, kissed his brother-in-law warmly, and my mother hurried in with the meal. She had surpassed herself; the fish was sizzling, the bread hot and fragrant, the fruit piled artistically, the wine bottles plentiful. My little sister, Ione, flushed and breathless from running to and fro from the oven and the merchant, brought in the bowl and washed our feet. My mother picked out the best of everything and carried it on a platter to my older sister, Illyrica, who sat a little apart, and the meal began merrily enough.

At first it was all fishermen's talk: the relative merits of sea and lake fishing, the prices and taxes under Herod in Galilee. Then we exchanged family news and ate till we were replete, and at last there was a pause in the conversation. I wanted my uncle to talk to me again, so I picked up where we had left off.

"Uncle," I asked, "why did your four friends leave their boats and go off on a wild goose chase?"

"Ah!" replied my uncle thoughtfully, "That's

what everyone is asking down there. It's a long story, but there are strange goings on down in Galilee, and nobody knows what to make of them; don't know what to make of them myself; but to leave your boat and your net and to go off, without a penny, well! They must be a great deal more certain than I am."

"Who, Uncle? And why did they go?"

Everyone was interested now, and my uncle sighed, as though he found it hard to answer our questions. His face was grave and puzzled when he spoke.

"I adopted the Jewish religion in order to please my wife, but I'm not interested in all the talk. They've had prophets by the score, quacks and miracle workers, and I've never believed in any of them. When the rumors started about the fellow changing water to wine in Cana, I laughed with the rest, but I didn't laugh when my patron's only son fell ill in the big house on the hillside. He is a good man, a nobleman in the town, and I sell him fish privately. He and his wife waited years for this child. It was the light of their eyes."

"And what happened?"

My uncle sipped his wine as though he hardly knew how to go on.

"Well, the child fell sick of a fever. Every physician in the district was called in, but they came away shaking their heads. I took the fish to the kitchen as usual, where I usually have a drink and a chat with the servants and, sometimes, if I happened to meet him in the grounds, with the master himself. But that morning the place was silent and the maids and servants were weeping, for they all loved the child. 'The hand of death is on him,' whispered one of them. 'His skin is like fire. He lies in his mother's arms and knows nobody anymore.' And as I stood at the door I saw the master ride out on his horse as a man rides out to battle, galloping down the road, the dust from those great hooves screening him from view.

" 'Where is he going?' I asked.

" 'To Cana,' replied one of the servants. 'They say there is a miracle-worker in Cana, a Nazarene!' He spoke with contempt, but no one smiled and I turned away, shaking my head."

My uncle paused again. He seemed almost afraid to say any more. The whole family sat with their eyes riveted on him, and only I, who sat facing her, noticed that Illyrica had risen and crouched close behind them. I shuddered as I glanced at her and looked away for her eyes were huge and black and naked fear seemed to be staring out of them.

"Go on," breathed my mother.

"I did not go back for three days, but they said in the marketplace that the child still lived. On the third day I returned. The master stood in the garden, and the child was chasing a little tame dog and his cheeks were warm and rosy with health. I was bold enough to stop and tell the master I was glad."

"Did he tell you what had happened?"

"Yes; he was too happy to keep it to himself. He even had to tell his fisherman." My uncle laughed. "He had arrived in Cana, which is not more than twenty miles to the west, and it was not difficult to find the prophet, because everyone was following him around waiting to see what he was going to do next. The master told me how he had humbled himself to kneel in the road before him and besought him to come with him to Capernaum before the child died. It was already

12

the seventh hour.

" 'Go home,' said the prophet, 'Your child is alive.' "

"And he believed him?" gasped my mother.

"He believed him. Why or how, he could not explain. He only knew that the word was true and the man was in control. He rode home, singing for gladness, and arrived before sunset. When he came in sight of his house the servants came running out to meet him waving joyously. The child was alive; at the seventh hour something had happened. The fever had broken.

"His wife filled in the details. She was sitting with the child in her arms, bathing his dry lips, when suddenly the burning heat drained from his body and his racing heartbeat slowed. *This is death*, she thought to herself and began to weep. But he opened his eyes and looked at her and they were no longer bright with torture and fever, but bright with health and happiness. She kissed him on the lips, and they were moist and cool. He sat up smiling. 'I want to go and see the puppies, Mother,' he said and ran out into the garden. She followed him and looked at the sundial. It was the seventh hour, the hour when the prophet spoke."

There was a short silence, then my father said, "What is the name of this prophet?"

"His name? Oh, they call him Jesus."

2

We all leaped to our feet, overturning the table and even I, used as I was to Illyrica's illness, had never heard a shriek of rage and despair quite like the one she uttered at that moment. My father clasped her in his arms to restrain her, for these fits seemed to make her stronger than human. My mother shoved Ione behind the corn bin, and I seized a handful of fruit and shot out of the house. I ran until I reached the corner of the street and then I turned and saw my uncle following me with quick strides. I waited for him and, big strong man that he was, I noticed that he was trembling.

"Does she often do this?" he asked. He sat down heavily on the harbor wall, as though too shaken to stand.

"Oh yes; now and again. It's nothing to worry about really. She gets over it until next time."

"Your poor mother!"

"Oh, mother's all right. She'll sit and nurse her for hours. She's got nothing else to do."

I could not keep the bitterness out of my voice, and my uncle glanced at me sharply. "What do you mean, boy?" he asked. "She's got the rest of you to look after and the house to run, hasn't she?"

I shrugged.

"She'll hardly know we exist for days to come.

Ione does most of the work, and she's only nine." I paused, and then burst out, "It's awful at home, Uncle. No one matters except Illyrica and no one comes to see us because they are all afraid of her. I wish I could get away from it all and grow up somewhere else."

He laid his huge hand on my knee. "I'm off to Zarephath to see the cousins. Can you come with me?"

I shook my head regretfully. I had work to do on the beach, cleaning and repairing the net, tidying the boat, washing the baskets, and my father would have punished me most severely if I had neglected my duties.

"Well," said my uncle, "I'll be back tonight. I'd like a chat with your mother before leaving in the morning. Now, get to your work, boy."

I watched him stride toward the bay that led to the causeway. I wished I could have gone with him, for my cousins at the farm on the road to Zarephath were a merry crowd. There was no dark shadow over that home. I sighed and went down to the beach.

I stayed on the beach all day, for I had eaten well in the morning. I worked and played with the other fisher lads and, when the sun was hot overhead, I swam out into the blue Mediterranenan. Only when the sun dipped to the sea did I go home and then, as I had expected, my mother did not appear to notice me. She sat, absorbed, crooning over my sister who lay, apparently unconscious, on the mattress. I helped myself to a bowl of buttermilk and a hunk of bread and goat's cheese and lay down in the farthest corner of the room. My father had already left for the night and Ione was asleep. The room was almost dark when my uncle lifted the latch and walked in. My mother leaned forward and refilled the oil lamp so that the light kindled and flickered all over the room.

"Ione," she called, "get up, and get your uncle's supper."

Ione tumbled out of bed, rosy and dazed with sleep. She walked straight into the wall to begin with and then staggered toward the table and stood, looking round her stupidly. My uncle took pity on her and went to help her, and my anger flared up against my mother. Why should poor little Ione be awakened, while she sat idly rocking my pampered sister? Once again, I hated Illyrica.

I lay for a while watching the group and their shadows on the wall. My sister's face looked white and dead, my mother's distraught with weeping. I don't think they even remembered that I was there.

"Well, sister, how's the girl?"

"She is quiet now." My mother's voice was toneless.

"I knew she was strange and ill, but you never told me about these rages. For how long have they been going on?"

"Since she was a little child; about ten years. And, brother, it's all my fault."

"How is that? Surely sickness comes from God, or the gods, whichever you believe in."

"Not this sickness; she was born with a twisted foot and this grieved me. I thought, *Who will pay a dowry for a lame girl?* So I took her to a soothsayer, a witch in touch with occult powers. She muttered many words and peered in a crystal ball and cried with a loud voice and laid hands on the child. She asked a great fee and day after day I had to lie to my husband to get that fee. I sold most of my wedding jewels, and he still doesn't know."

"And what happened?"

"Her foot was healed in time; she was no longer lame. But the power of the soothsayer was an evil power, and it clung to Illyrica. I know now why the Jewish nation is forbidden by their God to have anything to do with witches and soothsayers on pain of death, for their power is an evil power. Touch it, and it touches you. Possess it, and it possesses you. From that day we haved lived in the shadow of evil and fear and nothing can deliver us."

"Can't you go back to the soothsayer?"

My mother shook her head, "Will evil cast out evil? No, brother, I have tried all. Physicians and apothecaries can do nothing. I have loved her as surely no child was ever loved before, for love is a mighty force, but the power of evil is stronger than any human power and it grows all the time. Sometimes I think it will envelop us all and drag us all down into darkness and madness—oh, my brother, I'm so afraid."

She was weeping now, bowed over the still form. Suddenly she looked up.

"Brother, that prophet you spoke of; do not mention him again. His name seemed to add to her unrest. She has muttered it several times today. 'Are you come to destroy us?' she whispers, and there is terror in her eyes. No doubt, he too is in touch with evil powers and he will possess that little boy as they have possessed my child. Have no more to do with him."

My uncle shook his head slowly. "There was no evil in that garden," he said at last. "Only a sense of great joy—and goodness—and light." He rose rather suddenly, as though embarrassed.

"It was scorching on the road to Zarephath,"

17

he said. "I'll turn in, sister. I'll sleep where your husband sleeps by day, with the fishing gear. Good night to you."

My mother lay down beside Illyrica; in a few minutes my uncle was snoring, and everyone seemed asleep. Only I lay wakeful and afraid. For if the power of evil was stronger than any power on earth, then we were all lost. The power would grow stronger and the shadow deeper and do what it would with us. I must escape and get away; I would go to the cousins on the Zarephath road or to my uncle in Capernaum. But they might insist on sending me back, for I was nearly a man with a job to do. My father was waiting for me to finish my twelfth year.

I thought of my silent, patient father, who always came home, and I wondered again what he felt about it. In all our years together we had never discussed it, and this was the first time I had ever heard my mother talk of it. Perhaps, one day, when I had grown to manhood, my father and I would speak of this thing together. I gave a great yawn. No trouble can keep a boy, who rises before dawn, from his sleep for long. I pulled the blanket over me and slept soundly.

My uncle left next morning after another hearty family breakfast, and I crossed the causeway to the mainland with him, and walked southward for a little way along the coast road. I would gladly have crossed the border into Israel with him, but after a few miles he laid his hand on my shoulder.

"You had better turn back now," he said. "Be good to your mother and your little sister, learn the trade and inherit the boat. Fishermen do not always live long. So farewell, boy. I will come again soon and see how things are going."

I kissed his hand and he swung ahead, leaving

me on the road by the marram grass and the sand dunes, depressed and disappointed. For he had not invited me to visit Capernaum.

Yet I took his words to heart and went home as soon as my work was done instead of loitering on the beach till suppertime, as I usually did. It was late afternoon when I reached our street, and the westering sun bathed the little town in clear, golden light. Ione was just coming from the well with her waterpot on her head and we walked together. Ione worked as hard as a grown woman, but she bore no grudges. She lived with the evil but it had never, so far, cast its shadow over her kind, happy spirit. She loved life and it had never occurred to her that she was badly treated. She was a child of the light, if ever there was one, drawn to goodness as a moth to the lamp flame.

"How's Illyrica?" I asked.

"Better," replied Ione cheerfully. "Today she sat up and ate some meat that our mother cooked for her. She is quiet, and she seems to have forgotten. But, Philo, we mustn't mention that prophet Jesus again. She seems to think he is coming to destroy her. But, you know, I really liked that story about the little boy, and I've been thinking about it all day. If he cured that little boy, why shouldn't he cure Illyrica, and why shouldn't he cure blind Astarte, down the road?"

I was about to repeat my mother's words about evil casting out evil, but I remembered that I was not meant to be listening, so I just said, "He is a Jew, Ione, and we are Greeks or Phoenicians. He would never come over our border. They call us dogs over there, and even Uncle's wife has never been to visit us. Besides, a prophet is a religious man, and our religions have nothing in common. Anyway, did you really believe that story?"

"Of course; Uncle wouldn't lie to us. Didn't you?"

"It didn't sound very likely. It could have been chance that the little boy got well just then."

I glanced at her. Her eyes were clear and smiling, and I saw that I had in no way weakened her faith. At the door of the house she put her finger to her lips and smiled at me.

"Don't talk about him any more," she whispered; "only when we're alone." We went into the house and ate our supper of porridge and squashy figs, and I thought angrily of the meat that had been roasted for Illyrica. The rich smell of gravy still lingered, but my father ate his porridge contentedly enough and went off at sunset. But, as he reached the door, he turned and remained quite still, looking me up and down, as though assessing my height and the size of my muscles.

"At full moon," he said at last, "you may come with me in the boat. That is the best time to learn, when the sea is calm and the air warm. When the sea is dark and the waves wild, I shall not have time to teach you, so you had better start now."

I was thrilled. Now I was a man; I could sleep in the day and go out at night. I need no longer stifle under the dark shadow. I turned eagerly to my mother, but the great news meant nothing to her for she was crouching over Illyrica, who moaned in her dreams like a lost spirit. Only Ione, who was laying out the sleeping mats, turned around and smiled. Yet, in spite of her smile, there were tears in her eyes, and I knew that she, too, feared the evil that was in our home and looked on me as her protector. When she had finished, I sat down beside her and put my arm round her, and we sat together while the sky in the window frame brightened to crimson and the noises of the little town, feet on the paving stones, laughter of children and barking of dogs, faded to silence and there was nothing to be heard at all in the darkening room, except the moaning.

3

I shall never forget that first night of full moon when I followed my father down the street and stood on the shore. The sun had just set, but the sky above the horizon was ablaze and all the colors, flame, mauve and purple, were reflected in the darkening waters. I, who loved beauty, could have stood in dumb amazement, watching the waves catch fire; but my father was used to the pageant and had no time to lose.

"Wake up, boy," he snapped, "and bend to the boat. It's time we were launched."

Oh, the grate of the keel on the shingle, the first lurch of the boat, water borne, the slap of small waves to the side and the darkening stretch of water ahead as the glory faded! I was happier than I had ever been before, for somehow I felt that I was leaving my shadowed child-life behind me forever. I was told to take an oar, and knew that I was strong and free and a man. As we surged forward into the great spaces of the deep, the wind ruffled my hair and soon the nightly miracle took place; the moon rose above the mountains and the dark water was transformed to flecked silver. The little town ahead rose, bathed in moonlight, and the drops of water on the net sparkled like crystal.

Even in the quiet, empty hours before dawn, when my head was swimming and my eyelids too heavy to hold open, my father would not let me sleep. He kept me busy with the oar and tackle, working as in a dream; and, as in a dream, I saw the pallor of the sky behind the morning star and the gray shapes of the mountains beyond the foothills. Then, somehow, we were rowing shoreward dragging a heavy net and the whole world of sea and distant land was a cold, misty gray. My head dropped forward, and I thought I was the boy on the beach, waiting for the boat, but my father poked me painfully and I woke with a start and knew that I was the boy in the boat, waiting for the beach.

And then it came; once again, the sea was aglow with the quieter colors of morning and the sun warmed our faces, scattering the mist, and the first long, long night was over. Then, at last, my father had mercy on me; picking me up in his huge arms, he threw me on the sand like a puppy.

"Go and eat and sleep," he said kindly. "We'll manage the rope without you today."

Oh, the relief of creeping into the outhouse, laying my head on the tackle and knowing no more! I slept till evening and woke, ravenous and happy, for this was the life I had longed for and this, I thought thankfully, would be my life as long as my strength lasted. From now on, the great spaces and depths of the sea were my home, my father and his crew my companions, and I could forget about my mother and my sister.

But the summer passed all too quickly; up in the hills, behind my home, the vine leaves turned golden and the pomegranates ripened and darkness fell early. The evenings were cold now, the seas often choppy, and there were nights of rain and gray, windy dawns. My father worked long hours, for winter was coming and winter was a hard time for the fisherman's trade. When the great storms churned the Mediterranean, the boats were laid up for weeks on end and we lived on our savings.

One night in November the north wind swept down from the Lebanon heights and there was a cold nip in the air. My father, waking from sleep, went to the door of the house and shook his head.

"We're not going out today," he announced. "Go and tell the crew that they can sleep easy."

I ran off on my errand, rather disappointed, for I had slept well and felt ready for work. I never felt afraid when my father was with me, and I had been looking forward to going out in a storm. But the lads agreed with my father and seemed relieved at the news and, having delivered my message, I went on down to the beach. The sea was a foaming, white-crested waste of water under a lowering, copper sky and I ran along the shore for a long way, while the screaming sea gulls rose in my path. I was in no hurry to go back home, for Illyrica was always strange and restless at the onset of a storm, as though there was something in her in tune with the wild elements. I remembered my mother's words, "There is no power stronger than the power of evil," and I thought of the power of wind and crashing waves, and, although my father had never believed in them much, the power of the gods; the Greek gods of my mother, and the old Canaanite gods of our country, figures of war, savage cruelty, blood, and vengeance. Who, or what, was in ultimate control? I was suddenly afraid and longed for my father. I turned and sped back along the darkening shingle toward my home.

I dozed lightly, for I had slept nearly all day, and I woke at once when Illyrica rose up at midnight and cried out that a great storm was brewing and great waves rising. The wind was still moaning from the north, and I shuddered at the despair and desolation in her voice. But my mother knelt beside her, soothing, comforting so I turned my face to the wall. But a little later I was conscious of a struggle and the door was flung open violently. Then I knew that Illyrica had gone out, for in these moods she was stronger than human and no one could restrain her unless my father chained her to the wall. She would turn south along the bay, cross the causeway, and wander all night in the hills, while my mother, buffeted by wind and rain, would stumble along behind her, waiting till she was ready to come home. Had my father been there, he would have gone with her, but he was still down at the tavern enjoying a night off with the other fishermen, and would not be home till early morning.

And I? I was supposed to be a man, and if I felt guilty about my mother following alone on the stony hillside in the wind and darkness, I pushed the thought from me; it was so easy to pretend to be asleep. Once again, hatred for my sister surged up in my heart and I almost hated my mother too, for her blind devotion to this evil creature. I would not get involved and if a storm was coming, I would rather be at sea than out on the hillside. I pulled the blanket over my head and, this time, I slept.

When I woke it was morning and my mother and Illyrica had returned, for my sister hated to go out by daylight. The storm had quieted and everyone lay sleeping. I slipped out of the house, delighting in the cold, fresh air. I looked up and saw that the great mountains of the Lebanon range were white against the pearl gray, for the storm had driven the snow from the northeast. Very soon the sun would rise and the heights would be too dazzling to look upon, and I had a whole day in which to do what I liked, for the boat was ready for launching and the tackle in order.

I decided to go and visit the cousins on the road to Zarephath and, if she was allowed to come, to take Ione with me, for she would enjoy playing with my aunt's younger daughters. My aunt, who was my mother's sister, had married a prosperous landowner, whose farm lay on a hill to the east of the coast road between Tyre and Sidon. On a bright, cold morning like this the walk would be a pleasure. My mother and Illyrica were still asleep, but my father was washing his feet in a bucket and seemed in an approachable mood. He glanced at Ione, who was already sitting cross-legged at the grindstone, grinding the wheat corn for our breakfast and, apparently, enjoying it for she sang as she worked. It would not take her long to prepare the flat loaves and bake them in the round, clay oven, already stuffed with grass and shrubs for burning.

"Take her," said my father. "She works hard for her age, and a holiday will do her good. If Illyrica was out last night she will sleep all day and your mother can go to the well. But be back in good time, boy, for I think we shall go out again tonight."

Ione was thrilled. She jigged softly up and down as she shaped the loaves and we sat by the oven, inhaling the fragrance of burning herbs and fresh bread. When all was ready, my father came and breakfasted with us and as we sat, just the three of us munching and supping the good food, there seemed no dark shadow over the home; only wholesomeness and happiness and the delight of keen appetites and bright weather. I wished it could always be like this, and I wished my sister dead.

My father gave me a basket of salted fish for the cousins, and we set off gaily enough along the bay, across the causeway to the mainland, where we turned north along the coast road. It was still early, and we met no one except the wife of the leper, descending from her carriage, while her servant stood by with a basket, but her face was veiled and she did not even glance at us. The leper lived in a booth on the hillside, and I gave a little shudder as I saw his robed figure appear at the door, but I soon forgot him, for to our left lay the shore, the dunes, the driftwood and the bright tossing sea, while to our right, the countryside was still beautiful where the land, softened by the former rains, rose to the hills, misted by the first growth of grass. Here and there autumn still flamed with the browns and crimsons of the drought but the leafless crocuses had already sprung up, and Ione ran from side to side of the road, picking the delicate mauve flowers. I strode along at my own pace, thinking my own thoughts but her joy was infectious and I found myself smiling. I had never realized before how beautiful my little sister was, fairer than most children of our race. Her head covering had fallen off and was tied around her waist and her hair, fast coming unbraided, was the color of dark honey; but I did not chide her, for she was only a little girl and I wanted her to enjoy herself.

"I wonder how that little boy is now," she said suddenly.

"What little boy?" I asked.

She looked surprised. "You know," she replied,

as though the conversation had only just broken off, "the little boy we were talking about, the one in the garden who was healed."

I realized he had been in her thoughts ever since and I took her free hand. "Come, Ione," I said, "You must walk more quickly or we shall never get there. You tell our uncle and cousins that story and see if they believe you."

She gave me a shy, sidelong smile. "I know it's true," she said softly. "I just know; and when I'm older I shall go and ask him to heal Illyrica."

We said no more, for the farm was in sight with the land stretching away behind it; stretches of rich earch, softened by rain, seamed with boulders and traversed by trodden paths. My uncle had already started on the early plowing, and we watched him as he trudged behind his two red oxen, yoked across their necks with a light beam of wood. He guided the one-handled plow, pressing with his whole weight on obstructing roots and clods, occasionally using his goad to prick the beasts in the right direction. It was hard, concentrated work, and he never lifted his eyes from the figure of his oldest son, who walked ahead, scattering the seed.

We did not like to interrupt them, so we walked on to the house where my aunt and the younger children came running out to meet us. My aunt would have been very like my mother, but my mother's eyes were haunted and my aunt's were clear and happy. They gave us a royal welcome and treated us like grown-up guests. A small daughter washed our feet, and an older sister brought great, frothing bowls of camel's milk to refresh us, with fresh leavened bread and platters of olives drawn from the salt vats, for the olive harvest was only just over. And while we ate we talked and exchanged family news. My aunt wanted to know all about my parents, but no one inquired for Illyrica. They seemed afraid to mention her name, and I did not mention her either.

The younger boys obviously much admired me when I told them that I now went out with the boat at night. I felt like a real man and was glad when, hearing of our arrival, my aunt's husband and oldest son hurried in from the plowing and joined the group. Ione had gone off with the children to see a baby camel; I was just describing a stormy night at sea, and much enjoying myself, when they all came running back, warm and laughing, and flung themselves down on the steps that divided the large living area from the lower quarters where the cattle slept.

"Ione says," burst out a small cousin, "that there's a prophet in Capernaum, where our uncle lives, who can make people well just by saying so. She says she's going to find him and ask him to heal our cousin Illyrica."

There was a sudden silence and a small shudder went round the group. I saw my aunt clutch the charms she wore round her neck, and everyone looked furtive and frightened. I felt angry and ashamed.

"Some people will believe anything," I said loudly. "It was just some child who happened to recover from a fever, and I was surprised that a sensible man like my uncle took it so seriously. And as for Ione, I think she imagines that the gods have come down to earth."

"She's not the only one; there's plenty are thinking that."

My oldest cousin spoke for the first time since greeting us. His voice was slow and lazy, but he was no fool. At eighteen he was a skilled agriculturist and merchant, and this year he had driven the camels to Damascus to sell the oil after the olive harvest.

"What do you mean, son?" His father turned and looked at him, for he knew that this keen-minded boy had long ago discarded the old Greek gods and the superstitions of the Canaanites.

"Just what I say, Father; Philo may speak contemptuously of this prophet, but he hasn't heard the half. The whole of Galilee is talking about him. I stopped at an inn and there were many Jewish travelers returning home from their autumn festival. One had spent some days with relatives in Capernaum, and he seemed a sensible fellow. He told of how not only the sick are being healed, but of how a young girl, the daughter of one of their religious leaders, had been raised from the dead."

There was an unbelieving gasp.

"Well, I'm only telling you what I heard," said my cousin, with a shrug. "They say he has power over life and death. Many seem to think that he is the great deliverer that the Jews are waiting for; many secretly hope that he will free the country from the dominion of Rome."

"They are fools if they try," replied my uncle shortly. "Have they forgotten what happened less than thirty years ago when they rebelled against Herod Archelaus? Three thousand murdered and about two thousand crucified outside the walls of Jerusalem! No, my son, it doesn't pay to plot against the Romans. If that is what this prophet is planning, he will fail."

"But if he is a god? If he has power over death, then perhaps he will have power over his enemies. Perhaps he is stronger than everything."

It was Ione who spoke, very softly and shyly, and my uncle turned and answered her as he would have answered a man, which I thought was kind of him, because Ione was only a little girl who ought not to have been speaking at all.

"Where is the god that is stronger than everything" he asked, smiling down at her flushed face and shining eyes. "They say the Jewish god was a great god and did great miracles, but his people are oppressed and in captivity and he does nothing to save them; nor have our gods of war and fertility saved us. The Roman gods have had their day; who acknowledges them now? They say now that the Emperor is to be worshiped in their place."

"Yes," agreed his son. "Philip the Tetrarch has changed the name of Pan's city, Panion, to Caesarea Philippi after the Emperor and the Tetrarch, and men say they are as evil as each other."

My aunt glanced at him nervously and my uncle frowned. It was dangerous to speak ill of the Emperor. Men had died for remarks like that. I sat there listening, thinking of that strange conversation I had overheard in the night; "The power of evil; it is stronger than any other power," my mother had said. I looked up at my uncle.

"Uncle," I said, "what power do you think is the strongest power of all?"

He thought for a moment and then answered me very seriously. "Our ancestors worshiped gods on the high hills and under the trees, and they even sacrificed their children to win the favor of the gods. But we forget them and ignore them, and what happens? The sun still rises, the corn still sprouts, day and night, seedtime and harvest never cease. If drought comes, men cry to the deities, but the rain does not fall and the olives and the vines fail. Some call it the work of the goddess of fertility, but I believe in the power of nature; the life of the earth that works as it will and takes no heed of man; the power that guides the stars in their courses and sends rain on the earth."

He gazed out over his fertile, cultivated land as he talked and might have gone on for a long time, but I gazed out too, and noticed the lengthening shadows of the olives. I jumped to my feet.

"We must go quickly," I said. "My father may decide to go out with the boat and I mustn't be late."

My uncle glanced seaward. "I don't think you'll go tonight," he said. "Look at the sky westward; there's a storm brewing."

I looked; there was a strange light over the sea although it was a couple of hours till sunset, and not a breath of wind. I could not be sure what my father might decide, so we thanked the family and said good-bye with real regret, for it had been a good day and we had enjoyed ourselves.

I walked fast along the coast road, for I feared to be late, and Ione trotted behind me. Once I turned to see that she was keeping up, but she was standing quite still looking out to sea. In spite of the quiet evening, the water was still rough from the night storm; the deep blue swell caught the afternoon light and the tossing spray glittered like hoar frost.

"Hurry, Ione," I called sharply.

She ran up to me, bright-eyed and breathless.

"But if he can really cure sick people and raise dead people just by speaking, then all the things uncle was talking about, like droughts and storms, don't really matter, do they?" she questioned. "I mean, he could put everything right, couldn't he?"

Then I knew that this strange miracle-worker had taken Ione's heart captive, and neither my teasing nor my arguments could drive him away. I walked on in angry silence, for it now seemed as though both my sisters were possessed; one, by the power of evil; the other, by I knew not what.

4

By the time we reached home the sun was hidden in clouds and the wind had risen again, buffeting us as we crossed the causeway, blowing dust and sand into our eyes. My father stood at the door, looking down the street, but he was not angry.

"Get some food, boy," he said abruptly. "We shall go out tonight. I've sent for the crew. The wind is a lot less strong than yesterday."

I changed into my fishing clothes and hurried down the street with my father, munching my supper as I went, and only too glad to leave the house, for Illyrica was in one of her moods, muttering and staring and beating her breast. She was still going on about some great storm; and as we reached the beach, where dusk was falling, and heard the clawing of the breakers on the pebbles and felt the salt wind on our faces, I felt a tiny thrill of fear and edged closer to my father. The men were staring out toward a bank of black cloud on the horizon.

"Storm brewing up from the west!" remarked one.

"It's not here yet," said my father, "and we'll drive back ahead of it. We'll only go out for a couple of hours and keep near shore."

No one argued as we launched the boat and rode out into the heaving swell, casting our net not far from land. It was a clear, windy darkness and we could see the pinpricks of light where the lamps burned all night in the houses. We worked in our usual silence and the fish seemed fairly plentiful.

It must have been about two hours after midnight when I suddenly gave a shout. The moon had risen behind the mountains and broken out from behind the clouds lighting the sea and there, right ahead of us, I could see a black wall of water about to suck us into its vortex. Everybody turned and looked in that direction, and a great cry went up as the crew fell to their knees in the boat, each calling to his separate god in the face of death. Only my father slipped across to my side and put his arms round me.

Then, a moment later, it was all round us; roaring winds and crashing waves that tossed and filled the boat as if it was a mere toy. I cannot say what happened next, for all was darkness and confusion and swirling black water and bitter cold, and the knowledge that my father was holding me with a grasp like iron, drawing me toward a broken fragment of mast. I seized hold of it, but it was only a light spar, too light to support us both.

"Hold fast, dear boy," he shouted in my ear. "The tide has turned and the storm will blow you shoreward. Keep looking toward the shore lights and the morning—and care for your mother." He let go; a great wave swept him away from me into the black void and I knew that I would never see him again.

In spite of the surging waves I managed to keep my head above water as I clug to my spar. I could see no lights now; everything was swallowed up by the night and the driving rain. But the tempest was blowing due east and I knew that, if I could hold on, I must, in time, be carried ashore. I thought of my fisherman uncle who had wished to die at sea, and I wondered if my father had wished the same; but I did not wish to die, for I was only twelve and all life, untasted, lay before me. I clung desperately, and cried out to what gods there might be to have mercy on me and save me.

Then, as I rose, gasping, on the breakers and fell, drowning, to the troughs I remembered the words of my farmer uncle; "I believe in the power of nature, the life of the earth, that works as it will and takes no heed of man." And I knew that he was right, for here I was at the mercy of the ultimate power that neither god nor man could tame; the power of the storm, the wind, and the waters and I, no more than a meaningless piece of driftwood. Then I fell into a great despair and cried out for terror and loneliness.

Only a very strong boy would have survived, but I, who had been on the net almost since babyhood, was a very strong boy indeed. Also, in spite of the tempest, the autumn weather was still comparatively mild and the water not yet bitterly cold. Although time ceased to exist, I suppose I must have been about four hours in the water and it seemed to grow darker. I had forgotten about the dark hour before dawn and only thought that the night would never cease, and that in the next moment I must sink into oblivion and blackness; but I never did, for my stiff fingers seemed welded to the spar and I longed with all my heart and soul to live; to feel the shore under my feet, to see my mother's face again (how could I have ever thought that I hated her?), to feel Ione's warm little hand in mine and the sun on our faces. Oh, life was sweet, and I'd never really known it! I kicked my numb legs and tried to swim in what I thought was the direction of the land, but I had lost my bearings and I only seemed to go round in circles.

Then I noticed something; the storm was abating. The wind had ceased its howling and, although the waves rose and fell, they no longer crashed over me. Instead of going down into the depths, I was being borne along on the tossing surface of an inky sea. My reason seemed to come back to me and I knew that this mighty west wind must be carrying me shoreward and also, because the night had seemed eternal, that, if I could hold on long enough, morning must come.

It stole in so softly, so cloaked in gray, that I hardly noticed it coming; only I suddenly realized that the water was brown and swirling instead of black. As I was borne to the crest of the next wave, I could see the hills, ghostly purple ahead of me, against a pale sky, and I struck out with all my might. Another great lift of the swell, and I could see the ravaged, twilight beach, very close. Shortly after, my foot touched sand and then I saw that many people stood on the sands of the bay, holding their cloaks around them, weeping and beating their breasts. I noticed too, that the beach was strewn with wrack and pieces of wood where the fishermens' huts on the edge of the shingle had been swept away by the freak storm.

It was gray daylight when I came stumbling toward the land and the people saw me. A great shout went up, and a dozen or so men ran into the waves to try and carry me ashore. They laid me on the sand and, a moment later, my mother's arms were around me and we wept together for my father. Then I was wrapped in dry blankets, given wine to drink, and carried home on a stretcher. Somewhere a fire burned and I began to feel my numb limbs again, and very painful they were. Ione was sitting beside me and I knew no more for many hours.

I slept and slept and lay between waking and sleeping for another two days and nights, my mind and body so battered and bruised that I could hardly open my eyes. I kept dreaming that I was tossing in a dark sea and the waves were about to engulf me. But whenever I woke from these nightmares, Ione was always there, ready to bring me wine or water or to attend to my needs, and to soothe and comfort me with her simple kindness and childlike common sense.

On the third day I woke early and struggled to my feet, almost paralyzed with stiffness. My mother and Ione had gone to the well, and Illyrica, huddled in her corner, seemed asleep. I crept out of the house and leaned against the doorpost like a feeble old man, holding out my hands and lifting my face to the pale, wintry sunshine. But my mind was clear and I stood there, feeling life stirring again within me, until my mother and Ione turned into the street. They walked gracefully erect, carrying the big clay pots on their heads, and my mother carried two leather buckets as well. They were glad to see me upright, but their eyes were red with weeping and, because I was still very weak, I crept back into the house and wept too, for the future without my father seemed dark indeed.

Much had happened while I slept, and while we breakfasted, we talked. My mother told me that, a few hours after I waded in, my father's body had been washed up on the shore and, during the day, two of our crew and some from other boats had been recovered. But not all had perished. Boats went out as the sea grew smoother and two men were picked up, clinging to a boat that had turned upside down. A few others swam in, clinging to wreckage; among them the fourth member of our crew, a young man named Hiram.

The hulk of the wrecked boat, also washed ashore, now belonged to me but I was too young to captain it so, for the present, it would be rented to Hiram, who would repair it and fit it. I would continue as a member of his crew until I was old enough and strong enough to pick my own crew and navigate my own boat.

I felt miserable; I had never like Hiram. He seemed to me a sly young man always out for his own ends and always arguing about his pay. My father had hinted lately that he was thinking of getting rid of him, and now he was my master. If it had been one of my father's friends, it would have been different, but Hiram! Yet he was the only one who had come forward and offered to take on the business. Once again, my youth, my helplessness, the loss of my father overwhelmed me and I felt, more than ever, like a straw, tossed by the careless winds of fate, in bondage to a master whom I hated, shadowed by an evil power at home. In my weakness, I almost wished I had perished in the dark sea with those I loved.

But life must go on. I had eaten and drunk well and my strength was beginning to come back to me. The stiffness was wearing off, and I wanted to see what was left of what was now my boat. I made my way to the shore, very slowly at first, but gaining confidence with each step. By the time I got there I was walking almost normally, but I was not prepared for what I saw. The beach was a shambles of wrack and wreck and seaweed, the ruins of the shore huts scattered like a great rubbish heap, and the very sea, stained and brown and churned. But I found what I was looking for; the mastless, rudderless hulk of what had once been my father's boat, and Hiram already at work on it. The sight of it unnerved me, and I spoke very foolishly.

"Kindly make a good job of it," I ordered, trying to make my voice sound as gruff as possible, and merely producing a squeak. "I shall be taking it over soon and I don't want any shoddy work."

He looked down at me with an infuriating smile. "Certainly, little master," he sneered. "As I shall be captaining it myself for a few years, I shall certainly make a good job of it. I was even thinking of inviting you to be one of the crew if you behave yourself. You haven't shaped badly for a youngster, but you've plenty to learn."

He was enjoying himself, and I was at his mercy, a mere child in years who would have to obey this mean creature for years to come, and how he would enjoy ordering me about! I suddenly had a wild idea of insisting on renting it to someone else; after all, it was my boat.

"I'll talk it over with mother," I replied grandly. "There are others who would be glad to hire the boat and we are still looking round."

He smiled again, and this time his smile was wholly evil.

"You may have to look a long way," he said softly, "before you find anyone who is willing to rent a boat from those who are in league with the evil one. You may count yourself lucky that I am not superstitious and am willing to take the risk."

I gazed at him, dumbfounded, and he saw that he had shaken me.

"Perhaps you haven't heard what people are

saying?" he continued, leaning toward me and still speaking very softly. "They're all talking about it, you know. They all heard that sister of yours crying by night in the streets about a great storm. Who invoked that storm? Your home is accursed, Philo, and your boat is unlucky. Who wants to sail with those who have traffic with evil spirits?"

I turned and went away, lest he should see that I was trembling like a frightened child. My legs shook as I tried to hurry, but, even in my panic, I noticed that no one spoke to me or condoled with me over the death of my father. People seemed to be avoiding me, turning down side streets as I came along, and now I understood why; the dark shadow had engulfed us all.

On reaching home I lay down, with an aching head and aching limbs; my mother sat alone for the neighbors feared to come and mourn with her. But I said nothing about what I had heard until evening, when Ione went to the well. It was the hour when all the little white houses in the street were flushed with golden evening light, an hour of peace and homecoming. But Ione returned much quicker than usual and we heard her footsteps running in the street; she hurried into the house and slammed the door, steadying her waterpot with her hand, and I noticed that she was trembling all over.

"What is the matter, Ione?" My mother and I both spoke at once.

"They said," she whispered, glancing fearfully at Illyrica, who was hunched in the corner, staring into space, "they said that it was Illyrica who brought the storm—they said that our house was accursed—they threw a stone at me and they said—" she buried her face in her hands and began sobbing. "They said that Illyrica must die."

I had an instant's vision of what life would be like if Illyrica was dead, but my mother's white, white face brought me to my senses.

"What nonsense is this?" I shouted. I had never before been so angry, and my anger made me strong. I forgot all my weariness and strode out into the dusk, down the street to the tavern by the shore, where the men of the village gathered of an evening. I pushed open the door, feeling several cubits tall, and stood in the midst of them. As soon as I entered there was silence, so I knew what they had been talking about.

"What's all this?" I shouted. "How should my sister call up a storm and drown my father who we all loved? My sister warned us of a storm, and we gave no heed to her words. Will you kill someone by whom the gods send warning of disaster? Shall she die, because we refused to listen?"

I looked straight at the tall, bearded tavern keeper in the center of the group, a councillor in the village, and a friend of my late father's. He nodded and turned to the others. Some of them looked thoughtful, others, frightened and uneasy.

"The babe is right," he said quietly. "Let us have no more talk of killing. Should we kill someone to whom the gods reveal the future? If she cries out in the streets again, let us listen to what she says and take heed."

There was a murmur of assent, and I suddenly felt small and shy, standing there in the lamplight with all eyes upon me. I turned and ran out into the comforting darkness with a light heart, for I had spoken as a man to men and they had listened to me. For the moment, at least, Illyrica was safe; but I wished, oh, how I wished, that my father's friend had not called me a babe!

5

There was no more talk of killing, but the whispering had done its work. Everyone in the village feared us, and people crossed to the other side of the street when they passed our house. The women seldom spoke to my mother when she went to the well, and the few visitors who came to our home came to offer us money if Illyrica could foretell the future, or even cast a curse on a rival lover. One man came offering to buy her as a professional soothsayer, but my mother, much as she needed the money, would have none of it, for she feared to stir up the powers of evil that possessed Illyrica. She soothed her and loved her, and sometimes when the restless mood was on her, she drugged her with wine and myrrh, and for a time the girl would seem quieter. She would crouch in the corner, her eyes staring and terrified, weeping and trembling for some torment that was coming to her, as though it was even now close at hand.

It was a dark wretched winter. The weather was often stormy with driving rain, and bitter east winds blew down from the snows of Hermon and Lebanon. There were many nights when it was impossible to fish and there was nothing to do but wander on the shore or sit in our accursed home. Other boys avoided me now, and when I tried to join in their games it was clear that they were uneasy. The loss of my father was a constant ache in my heart and I no longer looked forward to nights in the boat, for Hiram was an evil man and hired evil partners and they spoke of evil matters. Besides, Hiram had never forgotten my words on the shore and he delighted in treating me as a foolish child, making me do every menial, dirty job, often cheating me of my pay and my part in the price of the catch. There was no one to appeal to, and no one to help me; a kind of hopeless, sullen hate grew up in my heart, and I could think of little else. I spent long hours wandering along the coast toward the Sidon promontory, planning some distant revenge in the glorious future, when I would be grown-up and powerful.

We were poor too, for my wages were small, even when I got the proper sum, and Hiram paid a mean rent for the boat. Had it not been for the cousins, we would often have been hungry, but they were good to us and sometimes sent presents of corn, olives, raisins, bottles of wine or milk or oil. I would gladly have spent the idle days over at the farm, but even there I was not at ease. They were kind, but they treated us with a sort of nervous reverence, and my aunt kept fingering her charms and looking at us out of the corner of her eyes when we visited her, so that I was glad to get away.

In fact, if it had not been for Ione, we would have lived a lonely, isolated existence and known nothing of what was happening in the village or in the world beyond. But Ione seemed to break down all barriers, her friendliness and kindness reaching out like small tendrils making contact and drawing people to her. She worked very hard for a little girl, drawing water, picking bundles of grass and shrubs for the oven, digging edible roots on the hillside, cleaning, grinding and baking. But when her work was done, she visited her friends, received and welcomed where we were shunned and feared, because she was like sunshine that cannot be shut out, while we carried our shadows of sorrow and hate and fear with us wherever we went.

She spent much of her spare time sitting with a little blind girl who lived in a house near the harbor. Astarte had been born blind, but her people were prosperous and owned a big boat, and they had never sent her out to beg. On fine days she would sit by the open door in a patch of sunshine, lifting her face to the warmth and listening to the footsteps. She and Ione loved each other dearly and I would often pass and see them sitting there, their heads very close together, both talking, as it seemed to me, non-stop at the same time. One evening, as I was coming up from the shore, she ran after me and we walked home together.

"What do you talk about together?" I asked her, laughing. "You never seem to stop."

Ione looked away and then answered, very shyly, "I was telling her about that prophet, and we were talking about the little boy in the garden."

"Oh him!" I said. "Do you mean to tell me you are still thinking about him?"

Her eyes sparkled and she closed her lips rather tightly as though she was holding something back. But she was not very good at keeping secrets, and a moment later it all came pouring out.

"Everyone's thinking about him, Philo. That wasn't the only thing he did. You never talk to people so you never hear anything, but he has done many wonderful things and people are going to him from all over the place. Even Syrians are going to him; even from the coasts of Tyre and Sidon."

"Well, I should think they'd come back pretty quickly," I remarked. "He's a proud Jew isn't he? Can you imagine him mixing with Gentile dogs? You forget, Ione, it was a nobleman's son who this prophet was supposed to cure, and, no doubt, he got a fat fee for it."

She looked puzzled. "He's a Jew," she said, "but I don't think he's proud. The people who follow him are fishermen like us; and I don't think the people he heals are all rich people. Some of them are lame and blind."

I turned on her angrily.

"Oh, do stop talking rubbish, Ione," I snapped. "I may swallow a story about a child recovering from a fever; that happens every day. But whoever heard of a blind man seeing! It's quite impossible, so be sensible and don't believe every idle tale you hear."

She did not reply. She only smiled in a rather irritating way, and I could not help feeling that she knew more than she was willing to tell. But we said no more, for we both knew that the name of the prophet must never be mentioned in front of my sister, although I was sure that she often knew of what was never said, for she stared at Ione from her dark corner with wild eyes full of hate and fear.

It had seemed a long winter, but the bitter wind and driving rain never lasted for long on the Syro-Phoenician coast. We were fishing one night when I felt the soft breath of the west wind blowing from Cyprus and the islands and knew, with a lift of my heart that even Hiram could not quench, that spring was on the way. There was nothing to hope for, and yet there was a promise of hope in the air and the feeling stayed with me till sunrise when we rowed ashore and even when I climbed the street to sleep at home there was warmth in the sun and sweetness in the air. As for Ione, she seemed quite mad, brimming over with joy and mystery, singing little snatches of song when released from the house yet curbing herself when she went inside, for joy was something that vexed Illyrica more than anything else and, indeed, there was little enough of it in our home. My mother's sorrow and my heavy sullen mood matched her own and she took very little notice of me; but she was sensitive to Ione's restrained happiness and sometimes I wondered if she was going to spring at her and destroy her. It worried me, and one day, when Illyrica was asleep, I mentioned my fears to my mother.

She shook her head slowly. "I don't think Illyrica will ever hurt Ione," she said quietly. "She hates the daylight and if the rage comes on, Ione has only to slip outside as she has done many times before. And if the rage comes at night, well, don't I sleep with her in my arms? I would restrain her or follow her. Last time she went to the burying place and wept there all night, cutting herself with stones."

"But Mother, when the rage takes her she becomes twice as strong as a man. How can you restrain her? You should chain her to a stake in the wall, as others do. There's something about Ione that she hates; it's not safe."

I had never expressed this aloud before and I expected my mother to be angry. Instead, she remained silent but I could see that she was very troubled.

But in spite of the brooding shadow in our home, the spring was advancing like a high tide. At sea, the fish were spawning and the nets were heavy in the mornings. I had little time for walking for we were busy night and day, and to work for a master that you hate is hard labor indeed. When the catch was sorted and carried to the market and the nets clean and mended, I only wanted to sleep but I knew that, across the causeway, the almond blossom tossed in the breeze and the sheep were casting their lambs in the flowering pastures, and the good earth awaited the latter rains and the seed. Ione escaped whenever she could, lingering over her grass-cutting, radiant on her return, the very embodiment of life and spring and sadly out of place in our wintry home. Her suppressed excitement annoyed me and I tried to find fault with her.

"You seem to have forgotten your little blind friend these days," I said cuttingly one evening as she slipped into the house, her hands full of wild cyclamen.

She turned to arrange her flowers in a little clay pot. When, at last, she spoke, her voice was rather sad.

"Why are you always cross with me, Philo? I haven't done anything wrong!"

Because you are happy and I am wretched, I thought to myself. *Because you have found some joy that I know nothing about; because you refuse to let the dark shadow rest on your spirit.* But aloud I said, "Because you are such a silly baby and you don't care about anything," and I went off to my work, slamming the door behind me, and was more miserable than usual that night.

And then, one day about a week later, I understood. It was evening again and we were sitting quietly round our supper of fish and bread when we heard running footsteps outside and the door was flung open. Little Astarte stood on the threshold, her young brother laughing beside her; and she was looking, looking, her hands held out in front of her, as though she feared to collide with such a bewildering tumult of form and color.

"Ione, Ione," she cried. "Come quick and let me look at your face. I can see; Jesus healed me."

We all leaped to our feet, but it was too late. Those terrible shrieks of despair and anguish could be heard all over the neighborhood, and neighbors called in their children from play and slammed their doors. Illyrica had fallen on the floor, tearing at her hair and her clothes and I pushed the two little girls into the street and forced myself to go back and help my mother. My sister was banging her head and my mother held a pillow under it, calling endearments, comforting, pleading. But it was no good; over and over those blood-curdling yells of terror rent the quiet evening: "Jesus, Son of God, I know you—why, oh why, have you come to torment me?"

At last she slumped, motionless, as though her frail body could no longer support the strength of the spirit that possessed her. She did not even seem to be breathing and a great hope surged up in my heart that perhaps she was dead. But my mother, who was leaning over her, suddenly looked up, her eyes alight with relief. "She still breathes," she whispered. "She is alive."

I knew that she would lie in a coma for hours and it was nearly time to launch the boat, but

I went to the beach by way of the harbor in order to see what was happening at Astarte's house. There was a crowd of people around the door, and this time I pushed through the middle of them taking no notice of their scared glances. The house was full of neighbors, and Ione and Astarte sat with their arms around each others' necks. Ione was still rather pale and shaken, but Astarte had not been frightened. Having never seen anything before, the sight of Illyrica in a fit was no more alarming to her than the bewildering sight of someone walking down the street, or a donkey, or the waves breaking on the shore, or the sunset or a camel. Her father was speaking and the crowd listened, enthralled.

"There were crowds and crowds on the hillside," he said. "They had come from all over the place—from Judaea, Decapolis, Syria, Galilee, and from along our own coastline. The crowd was such that it was difficult to get anywhere near him, and I'm thankful we went in early spring for there was no shade anywhere. People were nearly fainting with the heat and the stench of sickness but they pressed on; and the joy of those who reached him was so great that it drew us on. Then, about the twelfth hour, not long before sunset, we reached him; at least she did. We were pushed back but his followers pushed her forward."

"But what was he like?"

"He looked to me like any other Galilean, but it was difficult to see. He was so surrounded and he was always looking down on those who knelt before him so we hardly caught a glimpse of his face. You had to be near him to see him. You were close to him, Astarte; tell us what he was like."

The child had been staring round at the crowds

and the movement in utter amazement but when her father spoke to her a faraway look came into her eyes. "I don't quite know," she said. "You see, his face was the first thing I saw. And when I saw him—well, I didn't want to see anything else. I wanted to stay."

"But what did he do to you?"

"He asked me if I wanted to see, and I said yes; and then, he touched me and I was looking up and I saw his face. And then, I wanted to stay."

"But why did you want to stay? Didn't you want to look around and see the world and your parents?"

"Yes—no—I just wanted to stay with him." She was only ten, and she could not tell us any more or explain further. She was worn out with endless new impressions. Her eyes filled with tears, and she ran over to her mother and hid her face on her shoulder.

The crowd turned back to her father. I knew that the boat would sail without me, but I just did not care; I had to hear. And the interest was such that nobody noticed me now in the waning light, and no one moved away from me. All eyes were on Astarte's father.

"Did you pay him?" asked someone.

"Oh, no. There was no question of payment; many of them were far too poor to pay. Right on the outskirts of the crowd were two lepers, veiled from head to foot and crying out that they were unclean. Everyone kept a good distance from them, and their shouting was drowned by the noise of the great mass of people. But, somehow, he must have heard them. Just at sunset he turned from the crowd and went over to them. He seemed unafraid of infection. He touched them both and said something that we could not hear; but they gave a great cry and flung off their filthy rags and stood there, stretching their clean limbs and praising God. There wasn't a scar on them. I saw them, for we were just leaving."

"A leper! Oh, let me get out!"

It was Ione who had leaped to her feet, her face radiant and was fighting her way to the door. She pushed through the startled crowd and left them muttering and glancing fearfully at each other. I thought I had better leave too.

I remembered the veiled figure on the road to Zarephath, who had walked past us without seeing us, and I knew where Ione had gone. I could not blame her, but I did wish, in the circumstances, that she would make herself a little less obvious.

6

The house to which Ione had, no doubt, run was on the other side of the town, beyond the bay. It was very naughty of her to run off by herself like that, but she had always been an impulsive creature. She reminded me of a little soaring bird which might sit on your hand for a moment, but you could not catch it or tame it. But, in any case, naughty or not, I wanted to know what had happened so I walked across the harbor and sat down on the sea wall overlooking the bay, for I knew she would return that way. It was too early in the season for trade vessels to be sailing the Mediterranean, but in a few weeks ships would throng the port and set out, on the fair spring winds, for Rome, with their cargoes of cedar wood from the mountains and oil and rich hangings from Damascus. But tonight it was very quiet, and I sat, swinging my legs over the side of the wall, and thought of the history of the town that I had learned, as a little boy, at my grandfather's knee. From this very port another Hiram had set off with his cargo of apes, ivory, and peacocks for King Solomon. Here, from the twin harbors, great fleets of ships would set off to the north and south, to sail to the utmost borders of the earth. The island's formidable battlements had stood impregnable, until Alexander the Great had destroyed the old town on the mainland and built his causeway and marched across to conquer. Tyre, the "crowning city," fell and now the dream had passed and the glory had departed and we were nothing but a fishing town with a small port. My future, which had seemed so grand, seemed grand no longer. The days stretched drearily ahead of me without respite; a curse in the home and hatred and humiliation in the boat. Once again, I wished I had died with my father.

But my thoughts were cut short by the sound of footsteps on the stones, and I looked up. Ione was being escorted home by a servant, carrying a basket, and I took charge of her and the basket. When the servant had gone, I pulled her down beside me on the wall and lifted the lid. It was full of almonds, raisins, figs, and honey cakes and I helped myself greedily.

"Whatever made you rush off like that?" I asked crossly, for she deserved some scolding. "Mother will be worried about you, and, anyhow, it's a shame for girls to run in the streets after dusk."

"It wasn't dusk when I went," said Ione, stuffing her mouth with raisins, "it was sunset. The water in the harbor was crimson and gold from the sky. And you know where I went, or you wouldn't have come here to meet me."

She laughed and snuggled against me for there was a nip in the air, and I put my arm round her, liking the feel of her warm little body, and we sat for a long time, talking and munching. The moon rose, sending a silver track across the water and we forgot all about our mother; but this was not surprising, because she so often forgot about us.

"Tell me what happened," I said. I was curious to hear her story, for Cyrene, the leper's wife, was a figure of tragedy and mystery, and, since her husband's expulsion from the town, no one, except her servants, had seen her face. She was the daughter of a rich merchant, and her marriage to the young heir of a fleet of ships had been the talk of the town five years before. But only a few months after the wedding, when she was carrying her first child, they noticed the dreaded white patch and he was pronounced unclean.

His parents built him a beautifully furnished pavilion on the hillside where he lived alone, his body rotting, like a corpse in a gilded tomb; and every day, wet or fine, she went to him, heavily veiled, with a servant carrying a basket, and left food and wine on a stone; and, once a week, she took the child with her, on a little donkey, and he waved to his father.

"Tell me what happened," I said again, when our mouths were less full. "Did you get in?"

She nodded. "I knocked at the door and a servant came. I said I wanted to see her mistress and she said her mistress never saw visitors and I said it was a message about her husband, the leper, so she went away and when she came back she told me to give her the message and I said no, I'd only give it to her mistress, and then she went away and when she came back she said, 'Come,' so I went."

Ione paused for breath.

"And then?" I asked.

"Well, I went and I told her."

"Yes, I'm sure you did; but what was she like and what did she say?"

"I told her about Astarte, who had been blind all her life and came home seeing; and I told her about the little boy and about the two lepers and how the prophet Jesus touched them. She wouldn't believe me at first. She said no one would touch a leper, and I told her how they had thrown off their rags and praised their god. I begged her to take her husband, but she said he was too weak to travel and I was only a child and perhaps I didn't understand. But she said she had heard that many were going and she would ask other people. Then she put her arms round me and cried and I felt so sorry for her, and I cried too. Then she said I could come again, and she asked me why I cared so much and I said I didn't know. And then she told a servant to fill a basket with good things and take me home. Then I went away and I had to walk a long way across the carpet. I have never been in such a big, beautiful room before."

"I wonder why you do care so much; other people don't."

She was silent for a time.

"I think that prophet must care very much, to go on and on making all those people better," she said at last. "You see, Philo, I think about him all the time. Sometimes I pretend I'm there with him, helping him make everyone well. I pretend I'm guiding a blind child to him or helping a lame person over the stones. But, of course, it's only pretend. But here, it's real, and when I tell someone about him and they go to him—do you know what I pretend then?"

"No, what?"

"Well, then I pretend he's pleased with me and he looks down and smiles at me."

She spoke steadily, but slowly and softly as though this was a joy almost too great to share. She was gazing out to sea and the moonlight was bright in her eyes.

"Look at that silver track on the water," she said suddenly. "Do you ever want to run into the water and swim and swim until you come to the moon? All alone, with the water dark on each side, but the track shining all round you? Wouldn't it be lovely, Philo, if you could."

I rose to my feet and pulled her up beside me, for I thought she was getting downright silly now; but I did not say so, for she did not often share her fancies with me. I felt grateful too, for she had lifted me out of my gloom and I suddenly realized that Ione was the only happy thing left in my life. But I only said, "We must get home quickly. Mother will be really anxious about you, and Hiram will be furious with me for not going out with the boat. However, he can wait till tomorrow."

She came along behind me, but she did not hurry and I knew that in thought she was far, far away; but whether she was running up that silver track or whether she was looking up into the face of the prophet, I could not tell. But when I turned to tell her to hurry, she suddenly cried out, "Oh Philo, don't you think we could take Illyrica to him?"

"Oh, do be sensible!" I said quite crossly. "Of course we couldn't. How would she get there? She can't even bear to hear his name mentioned. There's something about him that she hates and fears. Besides, what could he do? No power is stronger than the power of an evil spirit; I heard Mother say so. Illyrica will never be set free until she dies, so stop thinking about it."

She said no more and, before we reached the house, we met my mother setting out to look for Ione. But she did not scold her much, and I could see that she was not really thinking about us at all. She turned back to Illyrica, who rose up and snarled as Ione came into the room, and then cowered and cringed and moaned in the corner, like some evil, wild beast cowers before a bright arrow.

I went, as usual, to the beach in the morning to help draw in the net, and when Hiram, in a towering rage, asked me where I had been, I simply said I had other business. He was very angry indeed and, had I not been the owner of the boat, I think he would have taken a whip to me. But I saw no danger and was as impudent as I dared to be and strutted home, after carrying the fish, with my nose in the air.

I expected a bad night and arrived on the shore sullen and defiant but, to my surprise, Hiram's mood seemed to have changed. He was quite polite to me and I hardly knew how to react, for I longed to vent my hate but found no reason for doing so. The days passed, the world blossomed into high spring, the latter rains fell and the hillsides were like gardens. Out at sea, the fish continued to spawn and trade was good; but none of this seemed to me to account for Hiram's behavior. He appeared to have lost his desire to torment me and was almost pleasant. Yet, when he looked at me, I was sure that I saw the same cunning and malice in his eyes. I thought of the sinister calm and stifling heat that preceded a storm at sea, and I had a strange sense of some brooding disaster.

Something was happening at home, too. My mother kept going out which meant that, while I slept, Illyrica was left in Ione's care and this angered me, for I knew that my older sister hated Ione, and might easily spring on her. But I could not ask my mother anything, for I had never known her so tense and I sometimes wondered if the evil that possessed Illyrica was beginning to creep into her spirit. If I tried to talk to her, she seemed afraid of me, as though she cherished some guilty secret that I must never discover. When I questioned Ione, she was unable to help me much; she only knew that my mother went out more than she used to and always seemed afraid and unhappy.

Then, one morning, as I wandered home after a night in the boat, I saw Ione standing in the street, waiting for me. "Come for a walk," she said. "I want to tell you something."

We climbed to the dunes behind the fishermen's beach and sat looking across the stretch of blue water to where Sidon juts out into the sea. "Well," I said drearily, "what's happened now?" For I had worked hard and was half asleep.

"It's Mother," said Ione in a frightened voice. "They thought I was asleep. The soothsayer came."

"What did she do?" I was wide awake now.

"I don't know: I couldn't see. The lamp was lit, but everything seemed dark and horrible. I thought I was going to scream; Illyrica kept laughing. And the soothsayer was angry and Mother gave her money and she was still angry and wanted more, and Mother gave her more and more, and Mother was crying."

"Money? But where did she get money from? We've only got what I bring and we save precious little of that."

"I don't know, but there was lots of money; and when Mother goes out she comes back with money. And Philo, the other day, when you were asleep, Hiram came to the house and they whispered for a long time and he gave her money."

"Hiram? He came and sat in our house? But perhaps he was just paying the rent of the boat."

She shook her head. "It was much more money

59

than that," she said. "It was lots and lots of money. And when he brings the rent they always quarrel, and this time he was pleased. Philo, something queer is happening and I'm frightened; and I don't want to be there when the soothsayer comes."

I rose to my feet, very wide awake indeed.

"Enough," I said. "That Hiram is an evil serpent, and I am going to know what he's up to. Come on home."

I strode toward the house feeling my manhood surging within me, and pushed open the door with a kick of my foot. My mother started and turned round and my sister laughed aloud, but it was an evil laugh, far removed from mirth or joy.

"Mother," I said loudly, "what is all this about? I hear you have had the soothsayer here, and you said yourself that she was in league with the powers of darkness. Can evil cast out evil? And where did you get the money from to pay her? I know she demanded a large sum."

My mother rose to her feet and stood in front of Illyrica, as though to protect her. Her eyes were terrified and, at another time, I would have felt sorry for her; but there were things I had to find out and I pushed on relentlessly.

"The money, Mother! Where did you get it from? And what was that devil, Hiram, doing here? Did he give you money?"

She was trembling, and she clasped her hands.

"I had to have it, Philo. The soothsayer promised to release Illyrica. If she was released, the curse would be lifted, and we could all live again as a family. Don't you see, Philo, that I had to have it? And Illyrica seems happier today."

"Where did you get it from?"

"Philo, there is still some left, I only paid a part

for her healing. Hiram will still hire you, and some day we will buy another one. But, don't you see, I had to have it?"

I still had not quite grasped what had happened, or else, I would not believe it. I think I shouted at her and raised my arm as though to strike.

"Where did you get that money?"

She shrunk back. "I sold the boat," she whispered. "But the soothsayer said that, one day, she would—"

My father's boat! I think I would have struck her, but Ione suddenly flung herself between us, all caution forgotten. "Mother, Mother," she cried. "The soothsayer hasn't made her better. Oh, Mother, let's take her to the prophet, Jesus."

I knew what was coming as soon as the word was out of her mouth, but, later on, I found it hard to remember what happened next. There was that awful howl of despair, and Illyrica sprang at Ione, like a wild animal, knocking her violently backward with her head against the grindstone. I seized the clay pot and flung it at Illyrica, and then I think my mother flew at me in fury for daring to harm my sister, but I am not sure. I only know that the hate and fear in the room were like physical blows.

"My sister!" I screamed, struggling and hitting out. "Have I only one sister? Leave that fiend alone and look to Ione, before she bleeds to death!"

Then, somehow, we were bending over Ione, staunching her head wound with a towel and Illyrica lay in a crumpled heap on the floor, her thin, sick body exhausted, as usual, by the power of her rage. My mother was weeping as I had never seen her weep before and Ione, deathly pale, opened her eyes and tried to comfort her. "Don't cry, Mother," she whispered very softly. "When I'm better, we'll go to Jesus; Jesus doesn't cost anything."

I rose to my feet, Ione seemed to be recovering. The blood had caked her hair, but it seemed to have stopped flowing. I felt I could not stay another moment in this cursed house, whose very air seemed to stifle me; nor would I ever go back to the boat that was no longer mine. I put on my tunic and picked up my cloak.

"Very well, Mother," I said. "Since you have taken all that was mine, there is nothing to stay for. I'm going to work with my uncle in Capernaum."

I slammed the door behind me and stumbled out into the spring sunshine, blind with tears.

7

Often, since that spring morning, I have traveled the forty miles or so between Tyre and the Lake of Galilee, but I have never done so without remembering that first journey, when I, a boy of twelve with a broken heart, turned my back on everything that I had known and loved, and set out to make a new life for myself.

At first, my anger was so great that I thought of nothing but the wrongs I had suffered. I knew now why Hiram had seemed so different; he had nothing to fear from me now, and no reason to be jealous. I was in his power now, so he thought, and he was just waiting for me to find out, waiting his moment of triumph. Well, I had cheated him of that moment. Never, never would I call him master. He would wait in vain for me when evening came, for I would be far away, and one day I would come back, with money in my pocket, and scuttle his boat and ruin him. These wild schemes of revenge completely absorbed me, so that I crossed the causeway and started out on the southeastern trade route, hardly knowing where I was going and noticing nothing. In fact, I must have walked some miles before I began to realize what I had done and what I had left.

It came over me very gradually; I found my anger melting away into a terrible loneliness, and if I had not been so proud, I would have run home again. I turned and looked back; the coastline looked far away and I could no longer feel the sea breezes. The air inland was hot and stifling. I was crossing a plateau and on either side of the road, the fields were striped with the pale gold of ripening barley and the emerald of young wheat. Between the springing harvests were strips of bare soil where the plowmen followed the sowers, for the latter rains had fallen and the earth was soft for the seed of the late summer crops. On the rising ground behind the fields, white clouds of olive blossom misted the landscape, and, just ahead of me, the road wound up into the Syrian hills and met the sky.

It was a beautiful scene, but I found no pleasure in it. I was thinking about my mother now and my heart seemed torn in two, with fury at what she had done, and a yearning to turn back, run into her arms, and weep against her shoulder. But I was a man of twelve and could never again do that, so I plodded on with the tears pouring down my cheeks, my nose running, and my father's voice sounding very clearly in my ears. "Look after your mother," he had said, but my mother had betrayed him and sold his boat and wasted my livelihood, and all for Illyrica. And I hated Illyrica even more than I hated Hiram and wished her dead with all my heart. But I did not think of Ione at all; I dared not, lest I should turn back.

The road was uphill now, and I was so worn out with grief and anger and physical weariness that each step onward was a struggle, as though I was walking through deep, soft sand. I had worked hard through the night; my head was swimming and my eyes kept closing, but I struggled on for I imagined that, if I could reach the top of the hill, the air might be cooler.

I reached the top of the first rise and, sure enough, a breeze from the west stirred my hair, and I thought that it carried a salt tang of the sea. The farmlands had given place to fields of flowers, but the hilltop was bare, except for a few twisted junipers and acacias blown toward the land by winter gales. I was parched and feverish with thirst, but even this could not prevent me from wanting to sleep so I left the road and found a little hollow in the shade of a spreading juniper. But as I lay down, I heard a small gurgle and opened my eyes again; I was lying by a spring of clear water, bubbling up from under a rock.

It seemed like a sudden touch of mercy on my bleak, joyless life and it somehow reminded me of Ione and I wept again. I leaned over and drank and drank and then washed myself all over, rubbing away the sweat and the dirt and the salt until my body felt cool and healthy. Then I lay down comforted, pillowed my head on my arm, and slept.

There were not many travelers on the road. On previous days the highway had been thronged with immigrant Jews traveling home after their Passover festival, but today was the Jewish Sabbath, and the only people I had met had been Roman soldiers or our own Phoenician peasants. No one noticed me, curled up in the shade with the gnarled roots spread round me like sheltering arms. Once, in the evening, I was awakened by a scuffling near my head and I opened my eyes to see a deer and her fawn drinking from the spring. I waited until they went leaping away into the trees, drank myself, and snuggled back into my hollow. This time I pulled my cloak round me, for the air was fresh and cool, and I slept again.

All through that night I lay dreaming; the moon rose and blessed me with her light and the stars in their courses circled above me, but I knew nothing. When I finally opened my eyes, there was a white mist over the hills, birds were twittering, and my cloak was drenched with dew. But there was a brightness seeping through the mist and I knew that the sun was about to rise.

I felt well and strong and ravenously hungry. I drank at the spring and bathed my face. I must find some food soon, but apart from that pressing necessity I was in no great hurry. I had a night's wages in my pouch, and I supposed I would come to a village soon. So I sat on the hilltop and waited, while the mists fell apart like bright smoke and the land around me became visible, partly in shadow, partly bathed in early morning sun. To my left, I could see the line of the coast, sparkling against the horizon, and my own hometown jutting out into the sea. To the northeast snow, so dazzling that I could not look on it, still lingered on the Lebanese heights, while to the south, the long ridge of Carmel stood like a rugged sentinel overlooking the Mediterranean. Then I turned east and there, ahead of me, the rosy clouds of sunrise still hung above the great hills of Galilee. Never before had I seen such a splendor of light and sky, rolling hills and valleys, and I felt unutterably small, a meaningless speck in the vast panorama. I took a last drink, broke a crooked staff from the juniper tree, and set out to continue my journey.

There was nothing to eat on those hills; the barley was green and the fig trees still in blossom. But today there were many people on the roads, for the Sabbath had passed. When I came to the border of Galilee, and crossed over into Herod's

Tetrarchy, I was questioned by a guard at the immigration control point. But he was quickly satisfied, for the fishermen and peasants pass easily from one country to another and I stepped across with a little thrill of fear and excitement, for I was now a stranger in a foreign land. Although at home I spoke Greek, the Aramaic dialect was fortunately familiar to us all.

The great hills stormed the sky ahead of me, shimmering in the heat, and I walked slowly, for I was beginning to feel weak with hunger. I was coming to a village; a small collection of flat-roofed, white-walled houses rising tier upon tier, with a village street leading to a market square. There were not many people about; the men were out at the last plowing and sowing and the women and girls, having been to the well, were working indoors. The boys were still being taught in the synagogue, and I crept up the street rather fearfully, wondering what to do and afraid of the scavenging dogs. But, to my relief, I met a boy setting out for the highway carrying a big rush basket of flat barley loaves, fried fishes, and hard boiled eggs, for travelers on the road to buy.

I approached him cautiously, for he was bigger than I; I knew that not many boys were honest and my hoard of cash was small. But, once again, I experienced that touch of mercy, for his face was kind and he seemed in no hurry. He asked me where I came from, and when I tried to bargain for three barley loaves and a few fishes he took a small coin from my hoard and told me to sit down under the fig tree and eat. Then he went away and came back with a frothing pitcher of ass's milk for me to drink.

"I did not ask for that," I said, looking at it longingly. "I must save my money for later on."

67

"My mother sent it; it's a gift," he said carelessly. " 'Give and it shall be given unto you, good measure, pressed down and running over.' That's what he taught us, up on the mountain, and it's all the fashion now; giving, forgiving, sharing. The poor have never had it so good before; and as for the sick! Why, there's hardly a sick body left in the village."

"Who?" I asked curiously, gulping down the milk and enjoying my meal as I had never enjoyed food before. "I don't understand."

"Don't you? Well, you must be blind and deaf then, for they've been coming in crowds for healing from your part of the world; from along the coast as far as Sidon, so they say. But it was before the great crowds began to collect that he climbed up there one day." The boy pointed vaguely toward where the Horns of Mount Hattin rose steeply to the east. "All the district followed him, and it's quite a climb, too. You should have seen the old folk puffing and panting. He sat on a rock and talked, and I've never heard anything like it."

"Who?" I asked patiently. "And what did he say?"

"Why, the prophet Jesus, of course," replied the boy. "You should have heard him."

"Well, as I didn't, tell me what he said," I repeated, and if it had not been for the ass's milk, I think I should have lost my temper.

The boy stared into space and shook his head. "It was almost like a new religion," he said at last. "The rulers and priests hated it; nothing about sacrificing, or giving money to the temple, or, if he mentioned them at all, they were not important. It was all about being happy, speaking the truth, loving, forgiving. He sounded as though money and possessions did not matter at all; just trust and obey God, and don't worry. He called it the kingdom of God, but whether it would ever work, is a different matter. But it set people thinking; no one dares say much because the high-ups are so against him, but it's made a difference to the nobodies like us. People are kinder and more honest, and feuds have been patched up. You wouldn't have caught my mother giving away her ass's milk for nothing, before *he* came!"

I finished the meal, thanked him gratefully, and set off again on my journey, much refreshed. I had covered a good many miles since waking and now I felt I could cover a good many more. I climbed on doggedly and reached a high pass, and there, far below me, bathed in the late afternoon light that illumines every detail, lay the Lake of Galilee, a shimmering jewel in the cup of the hills with white houses grouped round the bays and headlands, while to the northeast Hermon thrust its snows ten thousand feet up into the sky.

My heart beat rather fast for I was nearly there. I was beginning to hate these mighty, rolling distances and towering mountains. The waves of the sea were kind and companionable, even the storms were familiar enemies, but these vast spaces and heights spelled loneliness incarnate. I started running down the road toward the lake; a few peasants passed me carrying fish hung on reeds, and the familiar sight of fish and the boats far below comforted me a little; but not much, for the air was sultry and my world of fresh winds, wide horizons, and free, untrammeled waters was far behind me. I swallowed a big lump in my throat and trudged on.

8

Down, down, down; I did not know that the Lake of Galilee lay far below my own accustomed sea level, but I did feel as though I was descending into a hot trench. On the hilltop, the earth was brown and bare, seamed with black basalt rocks between which thorn and cactus grew, but lower down the slopes were carpeted with flowers; narcissus, wild anemones, flax, crowfoot, and small, flaming tulips, for the spring and the latter rains had come late that year.

Down through the flowered meadows I went and into the shade of deep plantations of palms, olives, and figs. But it was not a cool shade, for the hot air seemed held in the foliage and I was glad to get out on to the upper slopes of the town, where white villas rose out of gardens of flowering shrubs. It was beautiful, no doubt, but, to me, it seemed overrich, overheated. I was sweating profusely as I dipped into the lower streets and wondered where to find my uncle's house. Then I remembered that my uncle was a fisherman and the most likely place to find a fisherman at evening was on the shore or at sea. Perhaps there was still time; I hurried down to the shingly beach and found three men launching a boat. When I inquired timidly whether they knew my uncle they nodded, without stopping their work, and jerked their thumbs toward the lake.

"Gone out this half hour," they said. "Back before sunrise."

"Oh," I faltered. "And where does he live?"

"In the street behind the synagogue; anyone will tell you." They leaped aboard, their oars struck the water, and they were gone.

I stood, irresolute in the twilight, on the deserted beach. I had never met my uncle's wife; she was a Jewess and I was a Gentile, and she might well call me a dog and refuse to have anything to do with me. Waves of homesickness swept over me leaving me cold and frightened. Besides, I was so weary after my long walk that my legs felt unequal to carrying me as far as the synagogue.

I would wait until morning and go with my uncle, for I knew that he would be kind. I waded into the lake and washed myself and drank from my cupped hands. The water was warm and brackish, but at least it was not salt. Then I spied a derelict boat moored on the shingle, and I climbed in and lay down. A tiny breeze from the lake stirred my hair, and as I stared up into the deep blue sky, the stars seemed to surface from its depth; the same stars that had shone down on us when I sailed with my father, that had guided us shoreward on dark nights, the stars that were, even now, shedding their benediction on my home, my mother and little Ione. I curled up in my cloak and slept.

And then, the rustling, the croaking, the splashing, the twittering, and the thin screaming began, and I opened my eyes and wondered where I was. I sat up and peeped over the side of the boat, slowly remembering. The water lay like dark glass, but there was a cold light in the sky over the eastern mountains; pink, feathery clouds

71

against gray. Then I ceased to remember anything, caught in the present moment of living sound. As the light increased, sound merged into sight and the darkness behind me became ghostlike trees, rustling in the dawn wind, and from their foliage came the twittering of countless, invisible sparrows and the brightening surface of the lake reflected the dipping of screaming swifts. A couple of kingfishers dived and came up with fish in their beaks while, high overhead, there was a clapping sound and I looked up at a flight of wheeling pigeons. A heron appeared from the reeds and stood on one leg, bill poised. This was no barren seashore, but a haven, vibrant with life, and a new day had begun.

The sun had risen above the desolate mountains opposite and the boats were coming in. Droves of camels and donkeys were being driven down to the water, and the beach was fast becoming a noisy place. I did not wish to be caught crouching in the boat so, when no one was looking, I slipped over the side and strolled along the shore, looking for my uncle. I found him quite soon, easing the net from the stony floor of the lake lest it should break while his crew hauled on the rope. I watched him for a long time, but he did not notice me.

The net was drawn, the catch sorted. My uncle loaded the fish into baskets, laid them astride the donkeys and turned to go, and a boy, who I supposed was his son, went with him. I plucked up all my courage, and pulled at his fisherman's coat. "Uncle," I whispered.

He turned sharply and stared at me, as though seeing a ghost, and, for a moment, I thought I saw fear in his eyes. But he steadied himself, laid a huge hand on my shoulder, and said, "Philo!

What on earth are you doing here?"

He spoke so loudly that a crowd collected immediately, hoping that he had arrested a thief and I stood, silent and ashamed, staring at the ground and suddenly unable to explain my presence. And my uncle understood. His grip on my shoulder tightened.

"Come home, lad," he said, gently enough. "You shall tell us your story there." And then he added, "Is my sister well?"

"She is well," I whispered, and we walked along the beach together with my cousin stealing inquisitive glances at me from under the basket he carried on his shoulder. We came to a tax collector's booth on the quayside, where a villainous-looking fellow weighed the fish and demanded tax payment on the catch, which my uncle paid with a very bad grace; and the shifty hireling of a hated system grinned broadly.

We pushed our way up straight, narrow streets, past the pillars of a newly opened synagogue. The town was full of life and bustle, but I hardly noticed it, for all my thoughts centered on one question: would I be welcomed, or would I be sent home and, strange to say, I hardly knew which I wanted.

We had reached the house; it was much larger than ours for my uncle was a prosperous man; behind it was a shed, with tanks and vats, where much of the catch was salted or pickled. The boy was dispatched to deal with the fish, and my uncle led me to where his wife and daughters sat kneading and grinding together.

"My sister's boy from Tyre," he announced. "He will stay with us for the present. Let us eat, Esther; the lad must be hungry."

There was a moment's silence and again I caught that flicker of fear as they stared at me and I knew, instinctively, that I was an unwelcome guest, a Gentile dog, in league with evil. But they treated me politely, and I was soon eating a delicious meal with them; a great boiled fish, lentils in cream, leavened bread and honey with a pitcher of milk. I was ravenous, but soon found my appetite dulled by the uncomfortable silence around the table. Only the boy who had carried the fish gave me a shy smile as he joined us, and I smiled back, feeling that I had at least one friend.

"Well, boy," said my uncle, when the meal was over, "before I sleep, you had better come and tell me what all this is about." He led me outside to a garden behind the fishing shed where it was shady, and I told him all my story and very small and foolish it seemed, now that my rage had given place to misery. I would have given anything to be home again.

But my uncle listened carefully and asked a great many questions; very soon, I found myself telling him everything; not only about the soothsayer and the boat, but about Ione and the blind child and the leper's wife, and the more I told, the more he questioned, and there was a puzzled look on his face that I did not understand. When I had told him all, he rose to his feet.

"How will your mother and sisters live without you?" he asked.

"They have the money for the boat," I replied sullenly, "as long as she does not give it all to the soothsayer. The cousins from the farm bring us oil and wheat sometimes and Ione digs roots. Besides, if you will let me work for you, I could earn a little and take it home from time to time."

My uncle considered. "I will go and visit your mother soon," he said, "but the spring's a busy time for a fisherman. I could do with another boy at present, until Joel is out of school. You may stay and help Benjamin for the moment."

On the whole, I was relieved; I clung to his great hand, promising to work myself to the bone, and he smiled, patted my head, and went off to sleep. I stayed for a time in the warm, scented garden, just resting in the fact that I was safe, at last. Even in my father's lifetime, I had never really felt safe, with that evil, crouching presence in the corner of the home, but here, in this sleepy, luxuriant little town, one could forget danger. There was no danger, no challenge, no fight. I lay down on the thick grass and closed my eyes.

And yet, I would have given almost anything, at that moment, for a deep breath of fresh, salt air and the sound of cold waves breaking on pebbles.

9

In spite of my first impressions, I soon discovered that Capernaum was an exceedingly busy little city, for the great Roman highway, that ran from Egypt to Damascus, ran through it and branched toward the Phoenician coast. The streets were a pageant of interesting sights: Roman cohorts, marching in rank, merchants from north and south, camel caravans carrying carpets from Babylon and unloading their wares at the hated custom houses. I especially loved market days, when the peasants came in from the hill villages carrying early fruit, butter, and eggs, and the fishermen held out great shining strings of perch and carp. Then Benjamin and I were allowed to join them and earn a few coins on our own.

Benjamin was my friend, the first real friend I had ever had, except Ione, and she was only a little girl. For Benjamin knew nothing about the dark shadow and treated me as an ordinary boy. He talked very little at home, but then, neither did my uncle, for there was a strained atmosphere in the house, as though there was some point of disagreement between him and my aunt. Everyone seemed extremely careful of what they said, and, for the first few days, I thought that it was because of me.

However, I discovered the real reason when I had been in Capernaum for about a week. The catch had been smaller than usual, for the net had caught on a jagged rock and many of the fish had escaped. Our work was quickly finished and, my uncle being asleep, Benjamin and I found ourselves with a good part of the day free to do as we pleased, and Benjamin knew exactly what he wanted to do; he would ask his mother to pack us some food and we would row across to where the Jordan river flowed into the lake, just south of Bethsaida. Here the water was milky green and the big shoals collected. We would take our hand nets and do a bit of fishing on our own.

My aunt grumbled a little and said there was plenty of work to be done if we cared to look for it, but we didn't, and I think she was really quite glad to get rid of me. She packed a reed basket with a couple of eggs and some flat loaves and we set off in high spirits. The fish course we would provide for ourselves.

We ran down to the beach and launched the skiff. It was a perfect late spring morning, and already the heat shimmered on the deep blue surface of the lake. Benjamin rowed first and I lounged in the stern, gazing across at the wild mountains of Gadara and Gergesa on the eastern shore. In the fierce sunlight they looked scarred with hot clefts and gashes, as though someone had slashed the rock with a knife. I shivered a little as I looked at them.

"Have you ever been over there?" I asked Benjamin.

He hesitated "I've fished with my father over there," he said. "And I was up on that hill to the north, the week before Passover."

"Oh? What were you doing over there?"

"We went to see the prophet Jesus. People went from all along the lakeside. Philo, have you heard

77

about the prophet Jesus?"

I laughed. "I hear of little else from my young sister," I replied. "People have been coming to him from as far away as our town, Tyre, and being healed. I hoped I would see him here, but when I asked your sister, Hannah, about him she became really cross, as though I'd said something bad. Is he a good man or a bad man? And by what power does he do these miracles? Any why mustn't we talk about him?"

Benjamin gazed at the hillside ahead. "I don't know," he said slowly, "but we're just arriving. Let's fish for a little and then I'll tell you what happened up there, and afterward. Only, you'll never believe it."

The current caught us broadside and we had to row hard to cross the entrance of the Jordan. We arrived on the eastern side hot and out of breath, moored and jumped gratefully into the water. When we had cooled down, Benjamin fetched his hand net. He was to wade in and I was to stand on the shore and watch. I stood quietly, my eyes glued to the water, as he threw the rounded, weighted net over and over again and drew it back empty. Suddenly a dark shadow clouded the green water.

"Throw to the right, a little farther back," I called and he flicked the net over to where I pointed. I knew he had made a heavy catch, and I waded in to help ease the net. Together we lifted it in and settled down happily to examine the haul. We had struck a real shoal of the fat lake fishes with their crested backs and enormous mouths, in which they carried their young. We packed them into the skiff, leaving a few for ourselves, and collected stones, dry sticks and grass to kindle a fire. We gutted our fish, laid them on the hot, flat surface of the stones, and flug ourselves down to eat.

I shall never forget that meal. The peace of the lake seemed to enfold us, the shining water, the sun on our bare limbs, the crying and twittering of birds round about us; the hills encircling us, the gleam of white towns and hamlets far away, rising to meet the woods; and, best of all, because we had risen early and worked hard, the smell of fresh, baked fish and burning herbs. We placed the fragrant pieces between our bread, and made ourselves comfortable in the shade of a tamarisk tree.

"Well," I said, biting deeply into the hot fish, "go on."

"You'll never believe it," said Benjamin simply.

"Well, let's try," I said pleasantly, stretching myself, for the heat was rising and I was in no mood for argument.

Benjamin sat clasping his knees and stared dreamily across the lake.

"All right," he said, "I'll tell you. It was the week before the Passover. The people were wild about Jesus, the prophet. Thousands of them followed him round wherever he went. Ordinary life seemed to stop for a time. The nets weren't mended, the seed wasn't sown, the stalls were closed. You only had to touch him to be healed."

"Did you go?"

"Not at first; you see, my grandfather is a Pharisee and works at the synagogue. He says this prophet is mad or bad or both, and we are to have nothing to do with him, and my mother agrees with him."

"But why do the rulers and Pharisees hate him so, if he heals people?"

"Well, he says some strange things. He seems

to think that tithing and washing your hands and doing nothing on the Sabbath, and all the little rules that Grandfather is so keen about, don't matter very much. He says that loving, forgiving, sharing, and speaking the truth are more important. Besides, hardly anyone goes to listen to them any more, and you could hardly expect them to like that, could you? And then, they are worried about this power that he possesses. Where does he get it from? Some of the rulers think that it is an evil power, given to him by the evil one, but I don't think so."

I stared at him rather fearfully and my mother's words came back to me; "There is no power on earth stronger than the power of evil." Then I remembered the radiant face of little Astarte, raised to the light, and the hate and terror in Illyrica's eyes as she prepared to spring. Could they have anything in common? I could hardly think so. And anyhow, Benjamin still had not told me what happened on the hill behind us.

"We were never allowed to go," continued Benjamin, "until that morning when the prophet and his followers came down to the beach and got into a little boat, and we heard him say, 'Let us go over to the other side,' and we watched the boat take off, with the Zebedee brothers rowing. But the crowds who had hurried from the town, just stood staring and some, who had brought their sick, began to cry. But suddenly, those at the end of the beach turned and began running north and the whole crowd followed, racing toward the Jordan river and Bethsaida; thousands of them; the estuary was black with them."

"And you? Did you go too?"

"My father and I and the crew seemed to be left alone on the beach, when suddenly, my father grinned and said 'Let's go too; I'd like to see this man in action.' One or two little stalls were still open, so we bought some food and launched the boat. There was a little wind and we hoisted the sail and got across sooner than most of the crowd, but the prophet was already surrounded. Most of the sick in the city had already been healed but there were a few who rose up at his touch; mostly we just sat and listened. He talked and talked; even the children were quiet."

"What did he say?"

"He talked about his kingdom. He called it the kingdom of God. I don't think that he wanted to push out the Romans, although some hoped that he would. He said, 'the kingdom of God is within you.' I think he meant that a man's life could be governed by truth and kindness and goodness, instead of by lies and hatred and evil. He wouldn't be rich, but he would find peace and his real riches would be laid up for him in the life to come. I can't remember it all, but I've thought about it a lot. But that wasn't what I really wanted to tell you. It was about what happened in the late afternoon."

"Well, what happened?"

"His followers were persuading him to send the people away. Some of them had come without food and had been there nearly all day. Jesus said, 'You give them some food.' One of them laughed, and joked about the price, but Jesus was not laughing. 'How much food have you actually got?' he asked."

"Everyone looked around. We'd been listening so hard we'd forgotten our food, but now my father pushed the packet into my hand. 'Give him that, if he wants it,' he said, so I went and gave it to him; only five barley loaves and two fishes, but he seemed glad. He told his followers to make the people sit down, and he held our food and blessed it and began breaking it up. He gave it to the disciples, who gave it to the crowd and then came back, on and on and on. Everyone was eating, everyone was happy, and when they had finished, they all gathered around and cried out that he should be their king. But he turned away and went up into the hills alone, and, in the end, they all went away. I just couldn't believe it, but it happened, right there on the hills behind me."

I said nothing. I did not believe a word of it, and yet, why should Benjamin be making this up? However, I wanted to hear the rest, so I merely told him to go on.

Benjamin looked at me out of the corners of his eyes. "The next bit's worse," he said. "You'll never believe the next bit."

"If I could believe that bread story, I could believe anything," I replied, "so you might as well tell me."

"Well, Jesus went away to the mountain up yonder, and told the disciples to go home without him. It was late by now, after sunset. We had stayed to help clear up, and we all set off together, they in their larger boat and we in our small one, and there were other boats too. My father had been glad to see his old fishing friends again, and we did not hurry. We were halfway across the lake when the storm struck and, Philo, I've been out in storms on the lake but never in one like this. You wait till you get in one! The winds come sweeping down through the gullies of the hills and, in a few minutes, the waters are all white and churning. Sails are useless; they'd be torn to ribbons and we couldn't row against it. We just tossed and bailed out the water and waited for death."

"I know," I said. "It was like that the night my

father drowned."

"Well, we would have drowned too, but, about the fourth watch of the night, something happened. There was a sudden silence, as though someone had locked up the wind. The moon shone out on to a calm sea. Nobody spoke; we looked across to the other boat. The night was so clear and bright that we could see the followers huddled together and someone standing in the prow with his hand stretched out."

"But you said you left Jesus behind."

"We did; he wasn't there when we started. We didn't believe it was he until we got to land, but we followed them to the Gennesaret beach and there he was. The others were all muttering together, 'What sort of man is this, that even the winds and the seas obey him?' "

"But how did he get there?"

"No one would say. But one of his followers whispered 'He walked on the water.' "

"I don't believe it!" I burst out.

"I knew you wouldn't," said Benjamin quietly. "But if it's not true, then he must have flown, and that's not very likely either. And, in any case, he stopped the storm. The waves just lay down."

I said no more; I had too much to think about. I remembered the words of my farmer uncle, "I believe in the power of nature; the life of the earth that works as it will, and takes no heed of man." And I remembered, too, my own feeling of utter helplessness as I clung to the spar that night, at the mercy of wind and water. Was there really a power stronger than the forces of the universe? And did this prophet really possess it?

But it couldn't be true; it just couldn't.

10

I soon settled down to life in Capernaum. I worked hard, cleaning and mending the great dragnet, gutting and salting the fish, carrying it around or shipping supplies in the skiff. Sometimes, when our vats were full, we would row a load down the lake to the pickling sheds of Tarichaea, and I longed to land at Tiberias and explore the dazzling new city and get closer to the palace, all built by the hated Tetrarch, Herod Antipas, for his own enjoyment. But Benjamin was not allowed to set foot in the place, for the town had been built on top of an old burying ground, and any Jew entering it would be ceremonially defiled.

Just as I had loved to explore the coastline and the hills around my own home, so I longed to explore the shores of the lake and as the summer grew hotter and the hours of daylight lasted longer, I occasionally found opportunity to do so. My aunt had accepted my presence, making the best of a bad job for her husband's sake, but, when her father joined us for a meal, it was quite clear that he deeply resented my presence in the family circle. It was bad enough for the poor old Pharisee to eat with my uncle, even though he outwardly conformed to the Jewish ritual. But I was a raw Gentile dog, and my very presence was enough to defile his food. So on days when he was invited,

I would slip away and eat my dinner in the shady garden at the back, much happier than I would have been sitting under his disapproving stare; yet I often felt homesick and vaguely wondered whether, all my life, I was doomed to be shut out and different.

It was on the day of some family celebration that I had my bright idea. We had finished our work early, for my great-uncle and several of the rulers of the synagogue would be coming to dine and my aunt and the girls had been baking for days. They were all rather tired and cross, and I felt I was better out of the way. I followed my uncle out into the street and tugged at his sleeve.

"Uncle," I whispered, "can I take the boat and go right away today? I think I'd better keep clear of all this."

My uncle nodded, and I think he would have been glad to have kept clear himself. "You'd better take some food," he said, and he went into the house and came back with a fresh loaf, a chicken leg and some sweetmeats. "There, boy," he said with a smile, "you shall share our feast."

I was delighted. It was still quite early and I launched the skiff and seized the oars, for I knew where I was going. Across the lake, a little to the south of where Benjamin and I had fished, lay the town of Kerza in the country of the Gergesenes. The towns on the other side of the lake were inhabited by Greek emigrants or those who loved the Greek culture, and it was said that they decorated their houses with beautiful statues. But the Jews counted all statues idolatrous and, here again, Benjamin would not have been allowed to come with me. Even worse, they kept large herds of swine.

Here, at the north of the lake, the eastern shore

was about six miles across, rowing slightly south. I rowed steadily and rhythmically and was not tired, for the air was fresh on the still surface of the water. I aimed to land north of the town and to eat my picnic on the seashore, although the landscape was desolate enough. In front of me, the cliffs rose steeply from the sea but I thought I might find shade in a cave or cleft, so I drifted in, moored the boat, and plunged into the deep water, swimming lazily downstream, parallel to the shore. On the higher ground among the rocks, I could see herds of pigs rooting near a region of hollowed-out tombs, where the dead were buried. Further on were steep, cultivated fields, where the harvest had been reaped and the gleaners were busy at work. Quite close to the lake, a man was watering a small vineyard and he waved to me.

I was lonely, so I swam in and joined him. He was a strange man; there were jagged scars on his face and limbs, as though someone had attacked him with a blunt tool, and fetter marks on his wrists. But his eyes were clear and kind and his manner friendly. I helped him carry water to his vine patch and, when we had finished, he picked ripe summer figs from his tree and we sat down in the shade to enjoy ourselves.

"What are you doing over here?" he said, asking the question as though he was really interested. And I, usually shy and surly, opened up and told him part of my story; how I had fled from home, and found refuge at my uncle's house, and how I, a stranger, had no part in their Jewish feasts.

"But why did your mother sell the boat?" he asked. "The fishing must be good over there on the coast. It seems a foolish thing to do."

I was silent. I found it very difficult to speak

about Illyrica. She was the shame upon our life, the dark shadow, the unmentionable blot.

"My sister has a deadly illness," I mumbled. "My mother wanted the money for the physician. But it was my boat; she had no business to sell it. And, in any case, her illness is incurable."

"And did you never take her to Jesus, the Master?" he asked simply. "I heard they were coming from the north and from the coasts. Did the news never reach you?"

"It's not that sort of sickness." I was silent for a moment; then I said, "It's nothing the prophet could cure. You see, she has an evil spirit."

I could hardly believe what happened next. Instead of the usual shudder and shrinking, the man laughed out loud, and all the joy of birth and springtime and sunrise and every new beginning, seemed embodied in his laughter. But I did not think of this at the time; I just thought it was the happiest sound I had ever heard.

"Can't cure her!" repeated the man. "Boy, look up and gaze on me."

I lifted my head, arrested, and stared at the great weals and scars on his flesh. Then I looked at his face, transfigured with joy, and saw the love blazing from his eyes.

"Boy," he said, "did you notice the caves in the rock, yonder by the burying ground?"

"Yes," I replied.

"Well, that was my home for many years. I was an ill-used boy. I hated my parents and I hated life. I sought to commune with evil spirits to cast spells on those who had wronged me. But you cannot possess the power of evil; it possesses you, and my bitter heart was a good breeding ground. From then onward, I lived in hell, my friends cast me out of the town, my home was the burying ground and the rocks; not one evil spirit, but many. Do not hate your sister, boy, pity her, pity her deeply, for her soul is already in hell."

I suddenly felt terribly afraid. "What do you mean?" I whispered. "What happened?"

"I can't remember what happened. Others have told me of the crying, the wounding, the chaining, and the cutting with stones. I only remember the desolation and loneliness of evil; everything turned from us. There was another demon-possessed man with me. Men fled from us and the beasts and birds took flight. There was no love anywhere—the demons had turned from love long ago—and no rest forever; only the eternal thirst and torment of knowing what might have been."

I shuddered and drew away from him. "There is no greater power than the power of evil," my mother had said. Then where were they now, these demons? I glanced behind me; the rocks rose sheer behind me, swimming a little in the noonday heat, but there was nothing else.

"Where are they now?" I muttered fearfully. "What happened?"

He looked surprised, as though he had expected me to know all along.

"What happened?" he repeated. "Why, Jesus, the Master, came, of course. He crossed the sea just for us. Evil cannot stand before him; he set us free."

I sat rigid and staring. "What did he do?" I gasped. "Tell me what happened."

He sighed, "I've tried to tell it all over the Decapolis," he said, "for that is what he bade me do, but no one quite understands. They were never in hell, and anyhow, I can't remember it clearly, only terror, darkness, and confusion. And then, suddenly, it was all over, and we were free. Sometimes it seems to me as though we had been bound in a terrible dungeon by wicked captors, until we had forgotten what fresh air and light were like. And then, the city was besieged and the captors fought for their lives, terror stricken, until the victor rode in and they fled, screaming, before him and we came out free."

"But—but—what was it like?"

He shook his head hopelessly. "I can't tell you; at least, you would not understand. I was sitting on the hill, and somewhere below me was a great rushing and snorting and splashing, but I did not notice it at the time. Someone had thrown a cloak over my naked, bleeding body and, for the first time in years, it seemed quiet. The mad race had stopped and I rested. Love was all around me, washing me like cool water, and the birds were singing. The raging thirst was satisfied and there was no more might-have-been, because everything had started afresh."

"But what did he say?"

"I don't remember. I only heard the screaming and the struggling. People tell me that he simply told them to come out, and, of course, they came. Everything in heaven and earth and hell has to obey when he speaks."

"What did you do then?"

"I fell at his feet and worshiped. The other man had gone. Then the people came running from the village, angry and afraid because the demons had entered into their pigs and they had all stampeded into the sea. They begged him to go away, but I clung to him and begged to go with him."

"What did he say?"

"I think he would gladly have stayed, healing,

loving, satisfying all who came to him. But they did not recognize him. They preferred their pigs. So he went away, but I think he left me to tell the news he had come to bring, if they would have listened. 'Go home,' he said, 'and tell your friends what I did for you, and how I had mercy on you.' "

"I've tried. I stood and watched the boat sail away and I felt that love and life and strength were leaving me forever. Then, for the first time since my childhood, I noticed the colors of the sunset over the hills of Galilee and the reflections in the water, the red anemones in the grass and the wings of a kingfisher. The goats came home in the dusk, but, instead of fleeing from me, they nuzzled my hand and when I walked into the village, children came running out to meet me and doors were open. He is the source of life and love and beauty, but we, who have tasted of the streams, will find them everywhere. We are the satisfied ones."

"And when you tell them, do they believe you?"

"Not many. They listen and wonder but they still prefer their pigs. No one can really understand unless, like me, they've been in hell."

I did not go into the town. I felt too shaken by what I had heard so I went back to the boat and fetched my picnic. I shared it with the man and he accepted his part gratefully, as though any pleasure was a new and beautiful sensation. I said good-bye to him with regret, for I thought he was the happiest man I had ever met.

I rowed home deep in thought, moored the boat, and walked to my uncle's house, hardly noticing the passersby. The feast was over, but some of the Pharisses and rulers of the synagogue were still gathered in my uncle's home, talking with my aunt's father. I did not like to go in, so I wandered into the garden and found the children gathered under the mulberry tree and in the center, a girl about my age, to whom Benjamin seemed to be paying special attention.

They seemed particularly merry, and I stood on the outskirts of the circle, shyly enough at first, but I gradually found myself being drawn in. The girl's laughter seemed to spring up from some hidden source of joy and, although she was taller and darker, she reminded me of Ione. Her eyes sparkled with fun and kindness and because of her vivid life, we all felt more alive, more aware, and happier. How such a creature could have any link with that dusty old synagogue, I could not imagine. But just as the thought crossed my mind, someone called from the house. The girl leaped to her feet.

"I must go," she cried gaily, "but haven't we had a good time? One day, soon, you must all come to my house and we'll have a feast in the garden." She was gone, skimming across the lawn like a sunbeam, and one by one the children drifted off to their respective parents. The girls went in to clear the feast, and Benjamin and I were left alone.

"Who's that girl?" I asked abruptly.

"That's Mary, the daughter of the ruler of the synagogue. She's very special."

I grinned. "It's easy to see that you think so," I said.

He did not smile back. "I don't mean that," he replied gravely. "I mean something special happened to her; she's different."

"What happened to her?"

"Well, you must never mention it in front of my mother or grandfather. He says it was all nonsense, and that she was asleep."

"Well, why shouldn't she be asleep?"

"She wasn't asleep; at least, all the people who were there in the house say she wasn't. And Jairus wouldn't have rushed out and knelt on the ground, weeping, if she had only been asleep. After all, he is the ruler of the synagogue."

"For goodness sake," I said crossly, "what are you talking about? Who was, or who wasn't asleep, and why is it so important?"

Benjamin swallowed hard and looked around to make sure that we were alone.

"Because Mary was dead," he whispered. "And Jesus took her hand and called her back to life."

11

I could not sleep that night. It was very hot and Benjamin, Joel, and I carried our pallets to the roof where the air was fresher. The two boys slept at once but I lay, hour after hour, tossing to and fro or sometimes getting up to lean over the parapet and gaze out over the water. The moonlight flooded the little city of Capernaum, gleaming on the white walls of houses and synagogues and silvering the lake. Night scents of stale fish, fried oil, and lake water drifted up on a tiny breeze and I rested my aching head on my arms and tried to think. But thoughts kept going around and around in circles, always coming back to the same point; and that point was the simple words of the man on the shore, "Go home and tell."

I had not really believed Benjamin's stories, but I could not doubt what I had heard on the shore of Gergesa. That had the ring of truth about it; that bit about the beasts slinking away, for instance. I suddenly remembered Ione coming home with a wounded puppy, a very young, floppy puppy who licked her face and nuzzled her chin as she carried it up the street. But, once inside the door, its body had become taut and tense and it had rushed into a corner, whining pitifully. As soon as someone opened the door, it made for the world outside, and we could not keep it.

"Go home and tell." I thought about my home;

my wasted, exhausted mother who might hardly notice me, if I did go; my tormented sister, crouching in her accursed corner, weeping, snarling, sometimes raving and exuding hate. And then I thought only of Ione who had believed from the beginning, a small candle in the dark, and I wondered whether the light had been quenched by now. Illyrica hated her goodness and sweetness, and would gladly have killed her. And I; I had left her alone, defenseless and in mortal peril, and perhaps it was too late now. Fear and guilt overwhelmed me; I buried my face in my arms and longed for the dawn.

I lay down at last and stared up at the fierce stars. What power guided them in their rising and setting, and what kept them on course? I suppose I must have slept, on and off, for the dawn stole in on me unawares, and I leaped up in the tender brightness of a summer morning. I slipped down the outer staircase, wondering whether I was late, for I wanted to catch my uncle on the beach.

The sun had not yet risen over the hills, and the world still lay in shadow. Benjamin would soon be down to help sort the catch and carry the baskets but, if my luck held, I might still have a chance to whisper to my uncle that I wanted to talk to him alone. And, sure enough, just as the first great brightness dazzled my eyes and made the peaks invisible, the boat grounded and the crew waded ashore.

"Where's that lazy son of mine?" said my uncle truculently. "You should have wakened him."

"He'll be here in a minute," I replied, and sure enough, I could see him, a fleet little figure, racing along the grass verge. "But I wanted to ask you something first. Uncle, I want to go home."

He looked down at me. "Just homesick? Or has someone been unkind to you?"

I shook my head, "Something's happened, I just have to go."

"Well," he said, "this isn't the time for talking. Hang on to the rope, boy, there's a good catch. Tell me about it up at the house. And, as for you, Benjamin, if you ever let the sun race you again, you know what to expect."

I worked hard, grudging every moment, longing to be on my way, but the shadow on the sundial in my uncle's garden had shortened considerably before the duties of the day were finished, and he had time to talk to me. But when, at last, we sat down in the shade of the fig tree, I was no longer in such a hurry. I wanted to tell, and I wanted to know.

"Well," said my uncle, "why home just now? Joel will soon be finished at the synagogue. Couldn't you wait?"

I shook my head. "Uncle," I burst out, "what do you think about this Jesus? Yesterday I met a man who said he had been possessed by devils, and Jesus healed him. If he has this power over evil spirits, then why not Illyrica? And where is he?"

"They say he has gone west to the coast." My uncle spoke uncertainly and slowly. "I hardly know what I think, Philo. Strange things have been happening round here, but you must never mention them in front of your aunt. The scribes and the Pharisees say he is possessed of a devil himself and does these things by the power of the evil one."

"But does evil heal and give life and open the eyes of the blind? This is a strange evil!"

"Give life? Who told you that?"

"Benjamin; he told me about Mary, Jairus's girl. Our cousin at the farm had heard it too."

My uncle shrugged. "She may have been in a coma; the sea may have quieted itself by a freak of nature; people often recover from sicknesses. But there must be something to draw men after him in the way that he does; Peter and Andrew, who lived down the street; the Zebedee lads, with their fine boat; even Levi the taxgatherer, though he was no loss. These were not women and children to be taken in by fables, these were my friends, men with prosperous trades. 'Follow me,' he said, and they rose up, left their nets, their boats, and their gain and went off after him. What did they see in him, and what power is this that can so draw men?"

I had no answer, and my uncle sat staring at the oleanders in full bloom above the well. I had never seen him look so troubled.

"But what do you think, Uncle?"

"I don't know, boy. A religion that teaches a man to be kind and just and honest is more to my liking than this endless washing of hands and, in any case, you can do no harm. Come inside, and we will prepare you some food for the journey. You had better start soon."

My aunt, obviously pleased to get rid of me, packed a bundle of loaves, salted fish, cheese, and olives and my uncle slipped some money into my girdle. "Take it to your mother," he said. "You have worked well and earned it," and I knew that he and Joel and Benjamin were truly sorry to see me go, and I was glad of this. They stood at the doorway of the home and I left them with a lump in my throat, for Benjamin had been my first real friend, as close as a brother, and my uncle had been a second father to me.

I climbed the hill above Capernaum, trying to take in that I was going home, and I did not know whether I was glad or sorry. I was going back to my spoiled career and my shadowed home, but I was also going back to my mother and Ione, to fresh sea winds and the smell of salt tides. At the same time, I was leaving what I had come to love and I stood on the crest of the first hill and looked back to the blue mirror of the heart-shaped lake and its surroundings. Over on the other side I had talked with the man whose body was so scarred but whose eyes were so clear and happy. To the north was the little bay, where Benjamin and I had picnicked on that sun-drenched morning, and the green, deep water where the Jordan flowed into the lake, and just below me, the roofs of Capernaum, the gleaming synagogue, the beach and the little ships at bay; then southward to Mt. Arbel and the robbers' valley with its strange caves; Magdala, Gennesaret, and the great, shining buildings and pleasure gardens of Tiberias. Yes, it had been a good interval in my life but I had had enough of it, for a time, and I turned away and climbed on toward the Damascus highway. There were many people and beasts on the road at this time of the morning and I felt strong and cheerful. At midday I sat down under a sycamore tree by the side of the road and enjoyed a good meal. I was going home.

I slept down in the valley that night, for I had become unused to the cooler air of the heights and I set out again with the sunrise. Fortified by my aunt's plentiful food, I had made good pace the day before and I wanted to cover as many miles as possible, before the morning grew really hot. I attached myself to a caravan traveling north with donkeys and camels, for I was very conscious of the money in my girdle. They provided protection, but not much company, for they were Hebrews and had nothing to say to a young Syro-Phoenician lad like me.

On we plodded, over the great bare hills of Western Galilee and the day got hotter and hotter. Then a moment came when we reached the last pass and here I sat down and let the caravan go ahead. For here, at last, the road ran steeply downward and there, at my feet, lay the coastal plain, golden with half cut harvest fields backed by mountains. The heat haze had risen and the view was clear; far away, I could see, turquoise against blue, the line of the sea.

There were no more fields of flowers, only brown scrub and great, blue thistles, but I got up and jogged on, for even though there was little shade on the plain, I was determined to reach home that night. All that afternoon, when harvesters and gleaners rested in the shade, I trudged on. When at last I reached the causeway, the sun was setting over the sea and the salt, life-giving breeze fanned my face. But I did not quicken my footsteps, for I was seized with a strange foreboding, as though I was about to come face to face with an alien power of which I knew nothing. I stopped and found that I was trembling.

Well, there was nothing to do but to go on, and when I reached our street the light had faded and the town was quiet. Behind bolted doors, little children slept and tired harvesters rested. The fishermen had gone out with the boats and the gulls had stopped screaming. I reached our house and knocked.

A girl's voice that I did not recognize answered from within. "Who is there?" she asked.

My heart thumped violently. Who could she be? Had my family had to sell the house and move to a hovel, or was my premonition right? Had the power in Illyrica broken loose and destroyed them all? In a panic I beat on the wood, bruising my knuckles. "It is I, Philo, son of Ethbaal, come home. Let me in."

The door was opened immediately by a slight girl who stood, hesitating, with her back to the light, so I could not see her face. She stepped aside as my mother and Ione ran to me, flinging their arms round me, embracing me, drawing me in; but I stood, passive and amazed, staring over their shoulders. The little oil lamp flickered in the draught, casting shadows in the room, but they were not dark shadows. The light played for a moment on the face of the strange girl, who stood quietly to one side, waiting to greet me; a girl with clear, happy eyes and a shy smile, and at that moment I recognized her. It was my sister, Illyrica.

12

I think I knew what had happened, but I asked very few questions that night. For all their welcome, my mother and Illyrica seemed like strangers to me, and I felt I was sitting in the presence of a peace in which I had no part. Besides, my head was reeling with heat and weariness, and I only wanted to sleep. I ate the poor meal they provided ravenously and then lay down, as in days past, on the unused fishing tackle. In the morning Ione would tell me everything. She at least had not changed, and, with this comforting thought, I fell asleep and when I woke next morning, I wondered if the whole thing had been a dream. I glanced fearfully toward Illyrica's usual, dark corner but it was empty and there was an unaccustomed neatness and freshness about the house. My mother sat with her back to me, grinding, and at that moment the door opened, letting in a great shaft of sunlight, and, with it, came my two sisters each carrying a clay waterpot on her head.

I stared at Illyrica; graceful and slender, flushed with sunshine and exercise. She came toward me and kissed me and, as she did so, I noticed the scars on her arms. Embarrassed, I blurted out the first thing that came into my head; "I'm glad to see you better, Illyrica."

"Yes, thank you," her voice was hesitant. "Yes—

he came—he healed me."

The deep quiet joy in her face awed me. I had seen that look before. I turned, almost roughly, to Ione.

"Ione," I said, "put down that water pot and come with me. I shall need you this morning."

She turned inquiringly to our mother. "What about the gleaning?" she asked. "Can I come later?"

"Gleaning!" I shouted. "Is that how you live? Are we as poor as that?" I remembered the money in my girdle and tossed it across to my mother. "My wages," I said. "That will keep us going until I find work. Come, Ione."

I walked ahead and she followed trotting, as usual, to keep up with my long strides. I led her to the olive grove where we could sit on an old gnarled root in the filigree shade of silver leaves.

"Now," I ordered. "You tell me everything. I want to know just what's been happening."

Ione clasped her knees, and I listened, almost without interrupting, for she spoke very simply, without doubt or questioning. After I had left, things had gone from bad to worse. The sooth-sayer came over and over again and my mother paid out more and more money, and every time he came, Illyrica seemed to get wilder. When the barley harvest started, they fixed a great bar on the outside of the door to keep her in, and my mother and Ione had gone gleaning, sometimes coming home to find Illyrica bruised and bleeding and the house a shambles.

"And, all the time, people were going to Jesus and coming back healed," said Ione. "I kept telling mother, but she would not listen."

"Why not?"

"She said it was impossible to take Illyrica to

him. If anyone mentioned his name she would shriek and curse or even try to kill us. But I kept remembering the little boy. Then, one day, when I went to the well, the streets were almost empty. 'Where have they all gone?' I asked someone, and they said, 'They have gone to see the prophet Jesus. He is coming up the coast road. They say he is going to Sidon.'

" 'What? Here, outside Israel?' "

" 'Yes, here.' I didn't even ask Mother. I left the waterpot at the back of the house and I ran. There were so many people waiting and when he came, there were so many around him, I could hardly see him. It was impossible to get near, but I stood on a rock."

"But how did you know which one he was, if there was such a crowd?"

She looked surprised. "Oh, Philo, you couldn't mistake him; he's not like anyone else. Besides, he saw me, standing on the rock, and he smiled. Then I knew."

"What did you know?"

"That he could heal Illyrica."

"But how did you know? Did you ask him?"

"Oh no; I could never have got through the crowd. I just knew. I can't explain. If you saw him, you'd know too."

She was silent, reliving that moment and I glanced at her. I was beginning to know that expression; she looked as though she had seen in his face, all that a child could ever want to see and I, with my restless, unsatisfied heart, felt angry and cheated.

"Wake up," I exclaimed. "What did you do?"

"I ran home and told Mother, and this time she knew I was speaking the truth. Illyrica was screaming and crying, so Mother put the bolt on the door and told me to stay outside. So I stayed and she went."

"What happened? Did he come?"

"Oh no, Mother went to him. She followed him up the road, crying and calling and, in the end, he stopped and spoke to her, and she knew too."

"But what about Illyrica?"

"I was really frightened, Philo. She seemed to know that he was near and I was afraid she would tear down the door. Everyone ran away, and I was all alone. And then, suddenly, there was a terrible shriek and then all was quiet. I thought she had died and I began to cry, but I dared not open the door. I just sat waiting till Mother came back."

"Was Mother afraid?"

"No; she had talked to him and she knew. Illyrica was lying on the floor with her clothes all torn, but she was asleep. Then we both knew at once. She wasn't muttering and moaning; she was sleeping quietly like—like we sleep."

"And what happened when she woke up?"

"I don't think she did, that night. I didn't wait. As soon as I'd seen she was all right, I ran."

"You ran? Wherever to?"

"Where do you think?" Ione's eyes were sparkling. "I ran to Cyrene, of course. I pushed in and ran to her room and told her to harness her carriage and take her husband to the road next morning and find out where the crowd had gone. I knew her husband would have to stay apart, but I told her to push right through and get to him somehow. She began to cry, but I wanted to get back home so I left her. But when I reached the bottom of the stair, I could hear her calling the servants."

"What happened when you got home?"

"Mother and Illyrica were still asleep, but

everything felt different. I slept too, and I wasn't afraid any more. In the morning our mother and I woke and I went to the well, but Illyrica still slept. I went gleaning alone that day."

"But why should you go gleaning? What about the price of the boat? Surely she did not give it all to the soothsayer?"

Ione shrugged her shoulders.

"I don't think Hiram gave her much money. He just gave her what he wanted, and Mother had to agree because she was so afraid the soothsayer would put a curse on her. But we've managed. Anyhow, when I came home, the door was open and Illyrica was sitting just inside. Mother had washed her and combed her hair, salved her cuts and bruises and clothed her in a clean white dress. She looked beautiful. I ran to her and she smiled and put her arm round me. Next day she came with me to the well."

"Did everyone run away?"

"Yes, but I ran after them and told them that Jesus had healed her and then they came back. So many have been healed and lots of people believe in him now. You can't help it, when the blind see, the devils are cast out and the lepers are cleansed."

"But was the leper cleansed?"

"Oh yes, I was just going to tell you that bit. Soon after I got in, two servants came to the door. They carried a roast, dressed lamb, loaves of bread, fruit, sesame seed cakes, and bottles of wine. And, do you know what, Philo"—her face dimpled with laughter—"they were all for me! They were part of the great feast they were having up at Cyrene's house, because her husband had come home, and they said it was because of me. We had a wonderful time. We called Astarte and her mother and father, and we sat nearly all night, talking and laughing and eating and drinking. I did wish you'd been there."

"Did Illyrica talk and laugh?"

"Not much; she's very quiet. She just looks at things, especially out of doors, as though she has never seen them before. She's almost like someone who has just been born, if you know what I mean."

I knew exactly what she meant; I'd seen others; the Gadarene, Mary, and now, Illyrica. But what was there really to be so happy about? My father was gone, we were desperately poor and, worst of all, that contemptible wretch, Hiram, had got my boat for next to nothing. My hate seemed to rise up and choke me and I knew that I, at least, could never be happy until I'd paid him back. I clenched my fists and kicked the olive tree. Ione looked at me in surprise.

"What's the matter, Philo?" she asked. "Aren't you glad that Illyrica is well?"

"Of course I'm glad," I answered roughly. "But there are other things in the world beside this prophet and some people don't seem to see farther than their noses." I got up and strode ahead, because I did not want to see the light die on her face or the quick tears of disappointment spring to her eyes. When I reached the edge of the grove I turned to see if she was following, but she had run off in the opposite direction, to glean with Mother.

I did not go home; my anger seemed to possess me. I was angry with Ione for running away, angry with myself for hurting her and so angry with Hiram that, had I met him at that moment, I think I should have seized him by the throat. Almost without knowing where I was going, I made for the shore, the place for which I had so longed when I sweated and panted at the nets at Capernaum. But the smell of the ocean had no power to soothe me. I kicked at the pebbles savagely, not looking where I was going, when a friendly voice said, "Well, Philo, have you come back to us? You've been away a long time."

I looked up quickly. It was my father's friend, the tall, bearded tavern-keeper, whose wise counsel had saved Illyrica's life on that terrible night after the storm. I kissed his hand politely and he laid it on my shoulder.

"Where have you been, Philo? I heard you had gone into Israel. Your mother and sisters have been in sore need of you."

I blushed and looked down at the ground.

"I went to my uncle in Capernaum. I've been fishing in the lake. I brought home my wages last night."

"That is good. Now you must stay and work for them as your father would have done. Will you go back to Hiram's crew?"

I sensed some slight anxiety in his voice, and I shook my head violently. "Never," I muttered. "He persuaded my mother to sell him my father's boat for a mean price. He knew she had to take what he offered. He's a thief and an oppressor of the poor."

The man looked thoughtful.

"And yet, he's a rich man," he said. "His father died not long ago and left him a good inheritance. He has bought two other boats; if you're going to the shore, you'll see them drawn up on the shingle. But I think you are wise to seek another master. He has an evil reputation and his crew hate him."

I thanked him and turned back up the street, away from the shore, which seemed, somehow, defiled for me now. I could not bear to see my father's boat, new-pitched and renovated, no doubt, in the hands of this evil cur. I noticed nothing on the way home for my mind was full of violent plans. I would pierce holes in his boat, I would ruin him. I would burn his house, I would cut holes in his nets and, if possible, in his throat as well. I reached the house tense with impotent rage and kicked the door open, to find Illyrica, her household tasks done, just getting ready to join the gleaners.

I would have been more in tune with the old Illyrica than with this quiet, attractive girl, who greeted me so pleasantly. "Come, Philo," she said, "you have not breakfasted, let me wait on you." And I, pleased that she treated me with the deference due to a man, sat down and let her bring water for my hands and feet, as a woman should. Then she set fresh bread and olives in front of me and poured out a bowl of buttermilk. Yet I was embarrassed for she still seemed like a stranger to me, and after a few moments, I motioned her to sit down with me. There was certainly no trace of embarrassment in her. She moved with grace and confidence and she looked me straight in the face.

"Has Ione gone to the gleaning?" she asked. "I suppose she has told you all that has happened while you've been away. But it's good to have you back, Philo; we need you."

"Ione has told me what she knows," I said slowly. "But there are still some questions I would like to ask."

"Then ask them, Philo," she replied. "All that I know I will tell you."

"Well," I said, "you were alone in the house when it happened. Can you tell me exactly *what* happened?"

She puckered her forehead, and I knew that she had nothing to hide. She would tell me all she remembered with truth and clarity. I thought of Ione's words, "She's like someone who has just been born."

"It's not very easy to tell, Philo, because, now that the evil spirit has gone, the memory of him is very confused. I only remember terror and fear and a kind of suffocating heat. That is what evil is like; it poisons the whole atmosphere you live in and dries up your heart. You thirst for what you know you will never have and you grasp at what you hate!"

"But what did you want?"

"I did not know until I got it. I'm like someone who has found a spring of cold water and drinks and drinks, always thirsty for more, yet always satisfied."

"But what happened?"

"I can't tell you. One moment it was all wildness and terror, and, the next it had all gone. I lay, bruised and bleeding on the floor, but I was alone. I was not only healed and empty of evil, I was filled with peace and I knew the evil could never come back, because he had touched me. Then I slept."

"What do you mean, my sister? Who touched you?"

"Why, Jesus, the Master, of course."

"Jesus? According to Ione, he never left the coast road."

She smiled. "Is it so strange, Philo?" she asked. "Did the Greeks see Demeter in bodily form? Yet they believe that the earth springs to her harvests at her coming. Did Apollo ever appear to them, yet, when they see the sunrise, they believe that

108

he drives his chariot across the skies. Have the Jews ever seen their Yahweh, yet they boast that he draws near to them and works on their behalf? And would he speak the word of power and leave me defenseless? No, his spirit of peace possessed me as surely as the spirit of evil left me, and this is a power far stronger than evil. I think it is the strongest power in the world."

I gaped at her wisdom. But, even in the grip of the devil, she had always known.

"But Apollo—Yahweh—those of whom you speak are gods," I gasped, "if you believe in such things. This prophet; they say he's a Nazarene."

She looked straight at me and smiled, and I'd seen that smile before and cringed from it, for no hate could live long in its presence. All the power of life and love and beauty seemed to flow from her as she spoke. "He is my God," she said.

13

The tide of our fortunes had turned. My uncle had sent my mother a lot more money than my wages warranted, and it was Illyrica, with her wisdom and foresight, who suggested buying a small loom. Collecting shellfish, extracting the purple juice, and dyeing fabrics was a thriving industry in Tyre, for kings and rich men all over the province wore purple as a status symbol, and the weaving of fine cloth in the home was quite a prosperous trade. The girls learned quickly, my mother more slowly, and when the gleaning season was over, and three women worked in turns on the loom, the money started to trickle in; slowly at first, but more rapidly as they grew more skillful.

My own situation was more complicated. I had come back to bring news that Illyrica could be healed and to support the family; but Illyrica had already been healed and, for a time, the family was supporting me, and I hated it. I had intended to go back to my fishing and help man a new crew, but I just could not make myself go back to the shore and the boats. I had questioned my mother and I knew that, in her terror at the soothsayer's curse, she had practically given the boat away to a man already rich. My hatred had increased tenfold, and I could not bear to meet him, morning by morning, lording it over his crew, mocking my poverty. I did odd jobs from time to time and went and helped with the last harvesting on my aunt's farm, but she had four strapping sons and they did not really need me. I came home weary and discouraged, for harvesting was hard work and I was not used to working in the heat.

And, even though my home was so changed, I was not happy; I was still a stranger. All my life in Tyre I'd feared the dark shadow and been shunned because of my sister; in Capernaum, I had been a Gentile in a Jewish household, secretly despised and ill at ease. And, now that the home seemed full of peace and blessing, I still had no part in it, for what agreement has light with darkness, love with hate, or healing and forgiveness with revenge? I thirsted for what they had found and yet I shunned it, for I felt that there was some price to pay and the price was too high.

It was Ione who finally solved my work problem, temporarily at least. Since the healing of the leper, she had become an even greater favorite with Cyrene, his wife, and often visited her, doing odd jobs in the home and returning with all sorts of gifts and delicacies. One evening she came running in, her eyes bright with excitement.

"Philo," she said eagerly, "Cyrene's husband wants to see you."

"What!" I exclaimed, "The leper? I'd certainly like to see him."

"He's not a leper; you know that. He's a very strong man now and he wants to see you."

I was curious. "I'll go now," I said. "The evenings are long. Where shall I find him?"

"Out in the vineyards until sunset. I think you'd better wash and put on a clean tunic. I think it's rather important."

"What do you mean?"

"You'll see." She would say no more, and I set off on the harbor road. Cyrene's husband owned an enormous estate, but during his illness an honest servant had kept it going. Being an old man, he had been glad to hand it back, in good repair, to his master.

I reached the great, white house and asked, somewhat timidly, for the master. I was sent out to the estate and met him, coming from the vineyard, carrying a basket of early grapes. I saluted him respectfully and introduced myself, and he told me to follow him into the house. When we reached the shade of the porch, he sat down and motioned me to sit too.

"So you are Philo," he said, "the brother of our little messenger of life."

He spoke simply and kindly, without the usual pomp and ceremony of the rich. I glanced up at him shyly.

"We can never repay the debt we owe your little sister," he went on. "But we want to do all we can. I understand you are needing a job. The season of the grape harvest is just beginning and after that there will be the olive harvest. You look a strong boy, and your father was known for an honest man. Would you like to come and work for me until the season is over?"

Wouldn't I! It seemed too good to be true, but I hoped my eyes showed my gratitude. I promised to be there at daybreak and hardly slept, for the fear of being late. Every day, at summer sunrise, I ran along the southern shore, past the bay, and arrived in the vineyard while the dew still glistened on the leaves and the bloom on the grapes was inviolate. I picked the huge clusters, laying them in the baskets with meticulous care and carried them up to the house on my head. It was hard work in the heat, but we had a merciful master. At noonday we ate and drank and rested under the heavy foliage of the fig trees, only going back to our work when the sun's rays slanted. It was usually dark by the time I got home, tired and ready to eat and sleep. I saw little of my mother and sisters, but my master paid me generous wages and we were no longer hungry, or very poor.

I did not give my mother all that I earned. Each time that my money was handed out to me, I put some aside in a bag, hidden under the old pile of fishing tackle, for I was obsessed with the idea of my revenge. One day I would be a rich man; one day I would ruin him and buy back my father's boat. I thought about it in the vineyards, under the fig trees, running to and fro across the bay. It was the great object of my life, and only in these wild daydreams was I really happy.

It was a good life while it lasted, but the days were shortening, and the harvests were ending. The sun still shone, the raisins and figs shriveled on the rooftops, the vine leaves burned russet, but there was little to do on the farm, until the first rains fell on the parched, pink earth and the autumn plowing would begin. My term of work was officially over, although I still went up, two or three days a week, to clean out the asses' stall or to water the camels.

Then the rain fell, the first snow fell again on the Lebanon range and the west wind stirred the sea. The weather grew stormy, the fishermen gathered in the tavern, and the boats lay idle for nights on end. I had plenty of time to spare on these wild dawns and I longed for the spray and the great waves. Knowing that Hiram would be asleep, for his excesses at the tavern were well known, I would run down the empty streets, along the deserted beaches, past the boats moored on the shingle and my dreams of hate and revenge would be as wild as the tempest and as wayward as the storm.

It was on one of these mornings that I noticed a boy, slightly older than myself, sitting in one of Hiram's boats, mending a rent in the sail. I knew him by sight and I thought he had probably taken my place in the crew. The boy looked sullen and my curiosity got the better of me. I called to him, and he peered over the stern.

"What are you doing?" he demanded, rather glumly. "It's a wild day for the shore."

"Oh, this weather suits me," I answered lightly. "What are you doing? Are you one of *his* crew?"

"Yes," said the boy and he spat and cursed. "So were you once, too, weren't you?"

"I was once; but never again! I'd rather beg and starve than man his crew."

"You were lucky to escape. I hate him too, but there's others would beg and starve if I left him. My mother's a widow and I'm her oldest son."

I was about to say that I was in the same position, but felt ashamed of myself and kept silent for I had not been so considerate as this ragged boy. But it was good to find a comrade in hate, so I heaved myself over the side of the boat and sat down beside him.

"Why do you hate him so?" I asked. "What has he done to you?"

The boy pulled up his tunic, showing a back covered with weals, some of them still raw.

"That," he said. "I carried the fish up to the market and the merchant said it was short in weight. He's always playing tricks like that, but they don't always bother to check when it's a big catch. This time he was caught out, so he said I had stolen it on the way to the market and he took a stick to me and nearly killed me. I could only hobble for days and he wouldn't pay me my full wage till I could drag on the net like the others. Oh, I hate him, I hate him! We all hate him. One day I shall pay him back."

I was thrilled. By myself, I could do little, but with an accomplice, whose purpose was as strong as mine, nothing was impossible. I clenched my fists and started to pour out my story.

"I hate him because he's a thief and an oppressor of the poor. See that boat? It was my boat, left to me by my father who was drowned at sea. My mother had debts she could not pay; my sister was possessed of a devil and the soothsayer threatened to put a curse on her unless she paid. Hiram knew, and he got the boat for almost nothing; the foolish woman took just what he offered. He got the boat as a gift, and left them to starve, for all he cared. One day I'm going to ruin him and get back my boat, because it's mine, I tell you, mine!"

The boy looked at me with interest. "Perhaps we could fix up something between us," he said softly. "I'll tell you what I'd like to do. Just before the latter rains, when the spring tides are running high, there will be stormy weather. The boats will lie as they lie now. Why shouldn't we come together at new moon and burn one of his boats; some wood, some pitch, some sulfur—"

My eyes sparkled. "Why not tonight?" I whispered.

He shook his head. "Not yet," he said. "He has just harmed me and he would suspect me. Let

115

him beat a few more of his lads first and cheat a few more of his customers and then there'll be more choice. Besides, we must collect what we need little by little. If we bought a bucket of pitch and lit it the same night, the merchant would put two and two together. Patience, my friend, patience! He's going to pay the utmost farthing for his sins."

I felt almost lighthearted as I walked home, no longer frustrated by the impossibility of my dreams, but with a real, tangible plan to work on. He was to collect the pitch, I, the brimstone and sulfur, and we were both to collect wood. He was to decide on our night of action and I was to hold myself ready. I had only made one condition; it was not to be my father's boat that burned.

I reached the house and found my mother alone at the loom, for my sisters had gone to carry cloth to a merchant. This was unusual, and I sat down beside her and took the cloth from her hand, for it was seldom that I saw her alone and, in spite of her foolishness, she was my mother and I loved her.

"Mother," I said abruptly, "stop spinning and tell me what really happened when you went to the prophet. Ione is only a child and Illyrica can't remember much."

She shook her head wonderingly. "It is still almost too strange to talk about," she said. "If anyone else had spoken to me as he did, I would have been offended. But he cannot offend, for all he says and is, is love. I did not understand at the time, but it has all unfolded since."

"But what did he say?"

"Nothing, at first. I was nearly mad with hope and desire and fear, and I followed the crowd,

116

screaming and shouting. I knew he was a Jew so I addressed him as the Son of David. Over and over I cried, 'Son of David, have mercy on me.' "

"What did he answer?"

"Nothing. He just walked on. His followers were angry with me. 'Send her away,' they said, 'she is crying after us.' But I wasn't crying after them, I was crying after him. At last he said, 'I am only sent to the lost sheep of the house of Israel.' "

"I thought so; and yet, he had healed little Astarte."

"Yes, I knew it was not what it seemed. I had used the wrong name and he was trying to teach me. As Son of David, he was sent to his own nation, but there is another name, a name that belongs to me and to all of us. By this time he was standing still and I pushed past his followers and fell at his feet. 'Lord, help me,' I cried.

"Then again, he said a very strange thing; 'It is not right to take the children's bread and cast it to the dogs.' "

I looked up indignantly. "He called you a dog?"

She laughed, half tearfully. "Oh, you can't understand, Philo, because you have never heard his voice. He was testing me; testing my love, my desire, my understanding. How much did I really want what he so wanted to give? What price was I willing to pay for it?

" 'Yes, Lord,' I replied, 'but the dogs eat the crumbs that fall from the children's table.' Bread or crumbs were equally blessed from his hand. Others might feel he dealt harshly with me, but I understood, and when I said that, suddenly all the barriers were down. Joy beamed from his face and his love washed over me. 'Oh woman, great is your faith,' he cried. 'Be it unto you as you will.' Then I knew that he was stronger than the evil power and that Illyrica was healed."

"Mother, what is this power, and who is he?"

She was silent for a time, then she spoke, very softly.

"I think that he is the greatest of all gods. I think his power is the power of love."

14

I kept closely in touch with the boy who had taken my place on the boat, and we planned our revenge with the greatest care. We were to choose a windy, moonless night when the water was too rough for fishing; but, at the same time, the weather must be dry, for a rain-soaked boat would not burn. The conditions were difficult, and the weeks passed as we waited, but, in the meantime, I had collected quite a good store of brimstone and sulfur, bought in small quantities from different merchants, and my friend was also doing well with his pitch. It was after the turn of the year, at the end of a bright windy day, when we met on the harbor wall. The seas were still too strong for navigation and the harbor was almost deserted.

"Well, Philo," said my friend quietly, "tomorrow night will be the new moon and very dark. If the wind holds and it doesn't rain, we might have a try."

"A try?" I repeated. "If we try, we've got to succeed; I'm not trying twice. And what if he suspects?"

"He won't; he has too many enemies. He cheats left and right and his crew hate him more than ever. Before it flares, we'll cut across the dunes and, when the flames rise, we'll join the crowd from the back of the fishing quarter. If we are there, at the back, trying to push forward, who's going to know that we were ever in the front? Tell me that!"

I couldn't tell him anything. He was older than me and much, much braver. He saw the fear flickering in my eyes and laughed.

"Well?" he questioned. "Do you want to come in on this, or don't you?"

"Y-y-yes," I stuttered, "of course I do." I tried to summon up all my old hate by reliving the time when Hiram and I had talked on the beach, when I had learned that my boat had been sold. I even sauntered along and gazed at it, from a distance, conjuring up the memory of those happy nights when my father and I had launched it together. But I went home more sorrowful and depressed than angry, and woke in the night listening hopefully for rain. But there was nothing to be heard but the sighing of the wind and the cry of a nightjar and I lay, shivering with fear, until morning.

Bright sun, high tides, new moon, and a steady east wind tossing the sea and lashing it into spray. The conditions were ideal, and my friend, Jabin, met me behind the village to arrange the final details. He had already been down the night before and hidden our equipment under a piece of canvas, with a pile of stones over it. He was extremely efficient and seemed to have thought of everything. We were not to be seen prowling in the streets; we were to hide in the dunes just after sunset and wait there till midnight. We would light the fire on the far side of the boat, leaving a trail of pitch and sulfur to catch the pile of dry wood, and, long before the flames had leaped, we would have doubled across the dunes and rejoined the crowd that would wake to the blaze, and run with them to the beach. It sounded foolproof.

And yet, my fear persisted. All that day I was unhappy in the company of my mother and sisters and thoroughly restless and nervous. Our house was a haven of peace these days, a kind of domestic altar to this unknown god, where every action seemed to be done and every word breathed in his name, but I neither belonged nor fitted in. Although none of them reproved me (indeed, I was loved and made much of) my dark, angry thoughts made me feel a stranger and an outcast and I knew that I often spoiled the peace by my surliness and bad temper. I was happier out of doors, especially in the stormy weather.

But evening came at last, cold, clear, and windy, and I slipped on my coat and went out. It was a homespun Galilean coat, made all of a piece without a seam. Benjamin had grown out of it and my uncle had given it to me. People in Tyre had admired it, and I was proud of it and wore it everywhere. I walked across the deserted dunes as the crimson banners of stormcloud over the sea paled to gray, the wind blew the marram grass horizontal and the sand stung my eyes. I was glad to reach the appointed shelter and crouch in the hollow. Jabin was waiting for me, cheerful and confident, and he seemed to have no qualms about our plans miscarrying.

We waited for a long, long time. In spite of the shelter, I was glad of my coat. Jabin had a ragged sort of blanket, small and light, flung around his shoulders and he looked distastefully at my garment.

"What have you brought that great, heavy thing for?" he whispered. "You can't run in it, and it's too heavy to tie around your middle. You can't leave it here either. We may have to go back a different way, and if anyone found it they'd recognize it at once."

"I'll tie the sleeves around my neck," I whispered. "Don't worry."

The hours crawled by. A slip of new moon rose above the dunes and the sky was ablaze with stars, but they did not lighten the blackness of the night. We could hear the wind moaning above us, the crash of waves on the pebbles and the rattle of their retreat. The colder it grew, the more afraid I grew, and the more cheerful Jabin grew.

"Perfect conditions!" he muttered once or twice, standing up to peer over the dune. "We can soon go now; dark and noisy as can be!"

I was half asleep when he gave me a sharp kick. "Come on," he whispered.

Crouching low, we crept to the place where we had concealed our ammunition. The pitch was heavy, and we had to make three journeys. We piled it, with the dry firewood, under the curve of the ship and sprinkled it with sulfur. In spite of the cold night, I was sweating profusely. I had taken off my coat and flung it down on the sand, lest it catch fire.

"Now," whispered Jabin. "Strike the flints while I hold the oil lamp. As soon as it's burning and in place, run!"

It took several tries, for the wind kept blowing out the lamp, but at last the flame burned steadily. Jabin thrust it into the trail of brushwood and poured a bottle of oil round it. There was a splutter and a crackle and we ran. But there seemed nowhere to run, for, in a few moments, the flames were leaping high above the boat and the whole area seemed illumined. In that terrible, revealing light we should have been seen, streaking over the dunes. Like a fox at bay, I seemed to be running in circles, seeking for some place, in earth or sea, in which to hide.

"Straight along the beach," hissed Jabin, "and up through the trees at the end. Come on!"

I hurtled down that beach, stubbing my toes on rocks, slipping on the pebbles, until I reached the margin of the glow and fell gratefully into the deep darkness of the tamarisk trees and knew myself invisible. But, as I glanced back, I could see lights at the entrance of the village and heard the sound of shouting. We dared not stop. Pulling ourselves by the branches, we mounted the dune and dropped down the other side and here we paused a moment to regain our breath. Even here, the flare of the burning ship cast a faint glow. Jabin stared at me.

"What have you done with that coat?" he asked sharply.

My heart missed a beat as I remembered. I suddenly felt dizzy and faint and could not answer.

"Did you leave it down there by the ship?"

I nodded.

"Then I'm not being seen in your company again." He leaped to the top of the next small dune, then turned for an instant. "If you're lucky, it will burn," he said, "but I'm taking no risks."

He was gone, and I was left, rigid with horror, in the hollow. If they found it someone would know it was mine, and Hiram would demand the utmost of the law. Tyrian punishments were cruel and many had died beneath the lash.

I leaped to my feet. I was burning hot and icy cold at the same time and I knew I had to get away. I could not go home again. If they had found my coat, they might soon be hammering on the door of our house, demanding that I be brought out. The extreme likelihood of its having been shriveled up in the great blaze did nothing to reassure me. Like Jabin, I was taking no risks.

I was running swiftly now, on feet winged by fear, making for the causeway and the mainland. Everyone awake would be on the beach by now, and the inmates of the little garrison most likely drunk or asleep. Nothing would be done about a burning fishing boat until daybreak, and by then—It was only just past midnight and I had many hours till sunrise. By that time I would be far away over the border into Galilee, up on the wild hills, where wolves and wild boars hunted on winter nights. I shuddered, but I still ran; the dangers ahead were less terrifying than the dangers behind.

When I reached the main road, I was quite breathless again. I rested for a few minutes and then continued at a steady jog-trot. I was beginning to collect my thoughts and I remembered myself, a child, setting out on that same road on a bright spring morning, angry and broken-hearted, to an unknown world ahead. I seemed to have grown years since that last journey and to have learned so much about the world ahead. Every now and then, I stopped to listen and look behind me, but all was quiet; no shouting, or terrible running feet. Even the wind blew less coldly as I traveled toward the shelter of the hills. My jogging slowed and I knew that the land was rising, but I was not so afraid now, for there were still some hours of darkness. By sunrise, I would find a hiding place and sleep among the rocks and bushes.

I was climbing wearily, when I realized that the world was stirring in its sleep. A cock crowed from a farm, suddenly and loudly, and other cocks replied. A fox, creeping home, barked quite close to me, and I looked up and saw the contours of the hills, black against gray. I looked behind me and saw the eerie blue of shadowed snow on the mountains of Lebanon and I knew that morning was coming.

I was far too cold to sleep without my coat, and I prayed to what gods there might be, to send a bright, sunny day. My prayer was apparently answered, for the sky turned pearl and rose and, looking westward, I could see a sparkle on the sea. I knew this road now, and I was older and stronger than when I had last made the journey. With luck, I reckoned I could sleep for a while and then jog downhill to Capernaum. The last lap of the journey would be warm, even so early in the spring, and I would sleep in the boat and present myself to my uncle in the morning. Once I had arrived, I was not afraid of arrest, for neither my mother, nor my sisters, would dream of giving away my likely whereabouts.

My mother and my sisters! I felt my throat tighten, for I felt that I had now cut myself off from them forever, and it was this prophet who seemed to stand between us. I almost hated him. I remembered the words of the boy in the village, "the important things—speaking the truth— loving and forgiving—he called it the kingdom of God." And I knew that neither he, nor his followers, would ever have burned that boat and run away. I felt alone, wretched, shut out, as one who had glimpsed the gate of the kingdom, but who could never enter in.

I looked up at the great, vast sunrise over the hills and found that the light was prismed and irridescent through my tears.

15

I lied to my uncle and told him I had come back because I could not find work. He took me in without any fuss, although I did hear my aunt grumbling about another mouth to feed, and a large one at that! But I had arrived at a good moment for it would soon be the peak of the fishing season. My uncle was doing extremely well, and the vats were stacked with dried salted fish.

"When the spring harvests are over," Benjamin told me, "my father will hire a team of asses or camels and take the fish down to Jerusalem in time for the Feast of Pentecost. I shall have to stay and look after the business, but he might take you, Philo. Joel is going in any case."

On the whole, I was enjoying myself back in Capernaum. The days passed quickly and it was now the most beautiful season of the year. All over the hills of Galilee, wildflowers bloomed in carpets; wild cyclamen, scarlet anemones, dwarf tulips, and marigolds, while up against the spring blue, the cranes were flying north in great, white droves. The Jewish Feast of the Passover was drawing near, and everyone was busy, scouring their houses, or washing their clothes. I wondered what all the fuss was about until, one evening, Benjamin and I sat by the lake, throwing stones into the water, and he told me the strange old story; the bondage of Egypt, the plagues, and the final terrible night when the angel of death passed through the land, passing over the homes where the blood was sprinkled on the doorposts and lintels; the night of their deliverance; the night of their nation's birth.

"We don't kill the lamb any more now, except in Jerusalem," said Benjamin, "But we still remember it. It had to be a very special lamb, white and pure and perfect."

"Why?" I asked. "The blood would have been the same, whatever the lamb looked like."

He looked rather shocked. "The lamb had to be pure, without blemish," he replied quickly. "You don't understand, Philo. Don't you remember the story? It was the lamb or me."

"What are you talking about? The lamb or you!"

"Well, I told you the story. When the angel of death passed by, it was the lamb or the firstborn son. I am the firstborn, and if I had lived in the days of Israel's exile, that lamb would have died instead of me."

I said no more, for I felt that I had violated some deep instinct. I had not realized before how much Benjamin's Jewish heritage meant to him, and I decided to be more careful in future, for I had come to love my cousin. I had not, at first, told him about my real reason for being in Galilee, but one day when we were on the beach, a couple of soldiers came clanking by and I instinctively ducked behind a boat.

Benjamin laughed. "Whatever is the matter with you, Philo?" he asked. "Anyone would think that you had committed a crime. Whenever you see a soldier, or an official, you disappear. What's it all about?"

"Swear you won't tell your father."

"I swear by Jerusalem."

So I told Benjamin the whole story and he listened gravely. "They won't catch you here," he said, when I had finished. "You say that no one knows where you are, except your mother and sisters. Half the world passes through Capernaum, and who's going to track down one stray boy?" Then he added, rather surprisingly, "Did it make you happy, burning that boat?"

"Of course," I replied quickly. "It was the best thing I ever did. The dirty dog! Wouldn't you have felt happy, if you had been me?"

Benjamin gazed across the lake. His eyes were dreamy and he did not answer at once. "I suppose so," he said at last. "And yet, I'm not sure. That prophet kept telling us that the happy people are the ones who forgive, and the peacemakers. Sometimes, I wonder if perhaps he was right."

I was about to make some cutting reply, but checked myself. After all, that prophet had transformed our own home and healed Illyrica. I owed him some gratitude. So I merely said, "Are people still talking about that prophet? Last year he was all the rage and, this year, I haven't heard anyone mention him."

"That's because you are still a stranger," replied Benjamin, "so you don't hear what people are saying. He went south for the Feast of Tabernacles last autumn, and all those coming up from Judea bring news of him. He has been to Jerusalem several times; others have met him east of Jordan and some say he lodges in Bethany. Some tell wonderful stories about him, but no one speaks openly. The Pharisees and the teachers of the law hate him. Some even say that, in Jerusalem, they are planning to arrest him."

"They couldn't," I blurted out, hardly knowing

what I was saying. "If he can heal sickness and cast out devils and even (although I don't believe it) calm the sea and raise the dead, then surely he is stronger than a few priests. He'd never let them touch him."

"No," agreed Benjamin, "I'm quite sure that he's safe; only—you can't help wondering, what was the point of it all? What, where, when is this kingdom he talked about? I can't believe we've heard the end of it, and yet, when they wanted to make him king, he went away into the mountains. He missed his great opportunity."

I did not reply. I did not really want to talk about the prophet, for his teaching and way of life were not for me. I had had my revenge, and of course I was happy. It was only when my family, or Benjamin, talked about him, that I had that strange feeling that had come to me as I trudged over the mountains, of being in prison and glimpsing an open door into light and joy and freedom. But I had turned away from this door because I feared to pass through it. There was a price to pay, and it was easier to stay in prison.

Yet I was half fascinated and half repelled by the solemnity and ritual of the Passover. My uncle had wished me to share in the feast, for the old scriptures commanded that "the stranger within thy gates, should partake," but Rabbi Nahum, Benjamin's grandfather, who was joining the party and blessing the ceremony, insisted that that rule only applied to Gentiles who had embraced Judaism, which I had shown no sign of doing. The debate was so fierce, that I decided to solve the problem myself, by disappearing on the eve of the feast. In any case, I disliked sitting under the holy, disapproving stare of Rabbi Nahum, who was in a bad mood that year, because, for the first time since he was twelve years old, he was missing celebrating the Passover in Jerusalem, having decided that he was too old and unwell to make the journey.

So, early in the afternoon, I slipped out of the house, and walked along the lake in the warm spring sunshine. It was very quiet, except for the plop of the water tortoises and the singing and twittering of birds. I wandered southward until I came to the slopes of Mount Arbel and peered, rather fearfully, up the Valley of Robbers to the caves which had, for so long, been the dwelling place of thieves and cutthroats. No one had dared to pass through the valley, until the king had let down legions of soldiers from the rocks above, and the murderers were routed. I did not really like the place and, besides, evening was closing in. I sat down on the flowered bank at the edge of the lake and dabbled my feet in the water. The sun had dropped behind the hills and the water lay smooth and gray. Soon, as dusk fell, the families would gather behind those closed doors. They would remember the death of the lamb and the sprinkled blood and celebrate the life of their firstborn and the birth of their nation.

I was glad to be out of it and yet, at the same time, I felt lonely. My mind went back to the strange old story, and I shuddered as I thought of the angel of death, hovering over those closed doors, waiting to strike. But death had already struck, the blood was sprinkled and the dark specter passed on; and, perhaps, the trembling mother clasped her boy to her, and wept with relief because he was safe. Yes, I suddenly realized, it would have to be a very special lamb to pay such a price.

I sat for a long time, for there seemed a strange

atmosphere abroad that night. The eastern peaks faded to gray, and I wandered home along the darkening lake with a heavy heart. I did not care what time I got back; their feasting was not for me. I felt rejected, shut out, and desperately homesick, and, as the darkness grew deeper, old memories came flooding back; my father's anguished voice as the last wave engulfed him, my sister's wretchedness and terror; Hiram's face, greedy and malicious, tangible evil in the form of the soothsayer, forcing my mother to pay; then I remembered the little dead lamb. Why should the innocent always suffer? I suddenly felt acutely conscious of all the fear and suffering and sin and rejection in the world, and I wanted to scream.

But I didn't; for the new Passover moon suddenly came into sight from behind a cloud and I looked up into a starry sky. The night was alive with other memories now; the peace in Illyrica's eyes, my mother's quiet joy, the laughter of the man across the lake, set free from the dominion of evil; the expression on the face of Astarte, when she looked up at her father and knew that the darkness had passed, the strength and cleanness of the leper who had been cleansed—and I suddenly knew that there was an answer to all the misery, a power and a joy stronger than all the powers of evil.

His feet had often trod the road where mine were treading, and it did not seem in the least difficult to imagine him walking across the lake. If he was victor over death, sickness and demons, then why should he not also command the winds?

Only fifty more days, I thought, *and perhaps my uncle will take me to Jerusalem. And then—*

perhaps—perhaps, I shall see him.

But did I really want to see him, and what would it mean? I was not quite sure. I was beginning to believe that he was king and conqueror; but whether, or not, my conqueror, was a different matter.

16

I did not hurry, and I arrived home in the small hours of the morning. I crept up the stairs, flung myself down on my mattress under the roof shelter, and slept instantly. When I awoke the sun was high, and I ran down and washed at the spring in the garden. Then I hurried into the house, feeling hungry after my long walk the night before.

There were visitors reclining around the table. Benjamin and his father had gone out, but Joel and his mother and sisters were still breakfasting with the guests. My aunt's sister had come up from Jerusalem to keep the Passover with her parents and was staying for a few days. She and my aunt were talking so hard and so earnestly, that I don't think they noticed my entrance.

It was quite a feast; and while all eyes were fixed on the visitor, who was halfway through some very exciting story, I sat down and helped myself to some flat, unleavened bread, some salted fish, dried figs and olives, and poured myself out a bowl of buttermilk; and still no one noticed.

"Four days in the grave!" she half whispered. "And it's true; many, many people saw it."

I pricked up my ears as I munched; this sounded interesting. What had been four days in the grave, I wondered, and what had people seen?

My aunt seemed shaken. She pressed her hands

together and her eyes were wide and angry. "I don't believe it," she said. "I just don't believe it."

"Don't you?" retorted her sister. "Well, I do. You seem to forget, I married into the priesthood, and they believe all right. In fact, Caiaphas called an emergency meeting and my husband was there, and he told me—"

"But four days!" interrupted one of the older girls. "His body would have been corrupt after four days. It's impossible."

"That's what his sister said," replied her aunt eagerly, "but the prophet took no notice. He simply told them to roll away the stone and called out in a loud voice, 'Lazarus, come forth' and the dead man appeared, swathed in the winding sheet. Some people fainted, but the sisters ran forward. 'Loose him and let him go,' said Jesus, and Lazarus stepped out of his burial clothes, alive and strong."

And then I knew of whom they were speaking.

"But you didn't actually see it, did you?" breathed the younger girl, whose face had gone quite pale.

"No, I wasn't actually there. Bethany lies to the east of the city. But I have met many people who were there, and they all tell the same story. Hundreds are saying that he is the Deliverer, the Messiah we are waiting for, but of course if a national king arose now, the Romans would destroy Jerusalem, and nobody wants a repeat of what happened under Herod Archelaus. Caiaphas thinks that, for the sake of the whole nation, the man should be put to death, and I'm afraid most of the priests and temple rulers agree with him."

"But if he can raise people from the dead, how can they put him to death? He must be stronger than death, mustn't he?"

I had not meant to speak at all, I just wanted to go on eating, but the words seemed to have risen from my heart and spoken themselves, and I was as surprised as everyone else. But I was not prepared for the burst of anger that followed, as my aunt half leaped to her feet and made as though to strike me.

"What do *you* know about it," she shouted, clenching her fists. "You! A Gentile dog, pushing your way into our home and contradicting me and my parents! The man's an imposter, I say; a wicked imposter, in league with the devil. Get out of our house and don't sit there, defiling our feast."

I was scared, but I wasn't going to show it and, anyhow, Joel had hold of her raised arm and was soothing her. I rose to my feet slowly, helped myself to some fruit and Passover bread, and walked to the door. But before I left, I turned, looked straight into her crimson, distorted face and said loudly, "How very strange! He's in league with the devil and yet, he casts out devils. Is the devil warring against himself? Think about it again, Aunt."

I walked down the street, feeling rather pleased with myself, but by the time I had reached the shore, I was worried for, after all, I needed food and a roof over my head and she was unlikely ever to want me back. However, I hoped my uncle would stick up for me, if I kept out of the way for a few hours.

There was a holiday feeling in the air, for no one had fished on the night of the Passover and no one would fish on the eve of the Sabbath. I did not think I would be needed and I had a sudden great desire to go back to the place where I had sat with Benjamin, nearly a year ago, and he had pointed to the spot where the crowds had been fed, and told me about the storm. On that sunny morning, I had not believed a word of it, but so much had happened since then. I unhooked the boat and started rowing, aiming for that place beyond the mouth of the Jordan, where the water was green and milky and the vegetation luxurious. I arrived shortly before midday and scrambled ashore, but the Jordan, swollen by the melted snows of Hermon, had carried me to the south and I alighted close to a village where children were playing on a beach. Two of them were skimming stones across the lake, but the third had wandered a little way inland and was picking poppies.

I had only walked a little way, when I realized that something was happening. A thick cloud had risen in the sky, blotting out the sun. The sea, a moment ago azure blue, was suddenly gray and all the color had drained away from the flowers. I looked round, frightened, and saw, rather indistinctly, two of the children running toward the village. Then the cloud grew blacker—and blacker still; a moment later I could see nothing at all. That suffocating blanket of darkness had blotted out everything and I stood alone, stifled by its black silence. I lost all sense of direction; only the uneasy lapping of the water told me that the lake lay to my left.

I dared not move. I sank down on the ground and heard the terrified cries of that third child, not far away and seeming to come nearer. If he ran too fast, he would land up in the water and besides, even the company of a little child was better than nothing, just at that point. I stood up and called, as loudly as I could, feeling my way by the sound of his crying. His sobs grew less desperate as he realized that someone was looking for him.

"Where are you?" he cried. "Oh, please come; I'm here."

"Stand still," I called back. "Stay where you are and keep talking. I'm coming as fast as I can."

It took some time to find him, in that thick darkness that could almost be felt. I sat down and drew him into my lap, glad of the warmth of his sturdy little body, and he clung to me frantically. He was terrified and talked ceaselessly at first.

"It's night all of a sudden, isn't it?" he babbled, "and I thought it was only morning. They ran away and left me, didn't they, and why doesn't my father come to look for me? And when will it be morning again? It's a funny night, isn't it, because there isn't any moon or stars and it got dark so suddenly. I wonder when my father will come; who are you? Are you a man or a boy?"

"Just a boy," I replied, "and I'm sure your father's looking for you, but in this darkness he wouldn't know where to look, would he?"

"But, Boy, it was only morning; why is it suddenly night?"

"I don't know."

"Boy, do you think it will soon be morning?"

"I don't know; it was only about the sixth hour."

"Then it ought to be hot, and I'm so cold. When do you think the light will come, and why is it so dark?"

"I don't know."

He lay silent in my arms for a time, tired out by his own chattering. After a time he began to cry softly and I tried to distract his attention.

"Do you live in the village over there?"

"Yes, with my mother and father and my brother

and sister. They ran away and left me. Why doesn't my father come and find me?"

"He'll come soon. Tell me, did you go and listen to the prophet Jesus, when he talked to the crowds on the hills behind us?"

He stopped shivering and the dead, despairing weight of his little body seemed to grow lighter at the name.

"Oh yes, we all went; everybody went. My granny was lame, but she isn't lame anymore now. When it was evening, no one wanted to go home. Everyone was quiet and happy but a little bit hungry. He made us all sit down, and we had a picnic!"

"Tell me about that picnic."

He plunged into his story, forgetting the darkness and the fear. He had crept close to Jesus, and the man, who seemed to possess a power greater than death or demons, had smiled at him. Apparently all the children had gathered around. The little boy's voice grew dreamy as he tried to describe the events of that amazing day.

"You see, he loves little children very much." The child rested quietly against me, as though soothed by that memory of love and security. "He loves everybody—everybody—was happy."

His voice trailed away in sleep; I looked down and saw a soiled, peaceful, small face. I looked up, and, for a moment, the petals of the flowers and the water were gray. Then the light leaped upon us; not like a sunrise, cool and gradual, but suddenly, gloriously, scattering the dark, like a victor putting his foe to flight. I hid my face in the child's hair, dazzled, and a moment later, I heard a man's voice, calling frantically as he ran along the shore. I rose to meet him and laid the child in his arms.

138

His relief was so great that he hardly noticed me at first. He held his little son close and wept unashamedly for joy, for he had feared that his child had fallen into the lake. But, when he recovered himself, he explained very courteously that the other children had been bewildered by the darkness and had only just reached home, so he had been searching for them in the southern direction.

I could see by his dress that he was a rabbi but, unlike the pompous rabbis of Capernaum, he seemed a simple, kindly man and I dared to question him. I asked him what he thought was the cause of the darkness.

He hesitated, and a strange expression came into his face. "You are not a Jew?" he asked.

"No, I'm a Syro-Phoenician, but my uncle is married to a Jewess in Capernaum."

"Then you have lived for some time in Capernaum?"

"No, only for a short while."

He was silent, as though weighing his words. "You ask the cause of the darkness," he said suddenly. "I do not know; I cannot tell; unless, the words of the prophet Joel have come true."

He stopped and paced up and down.

"You forget, I know little of your scriptures," I said humbly. "What is this prophecy?"

He recited the whole passage in a deep voice, gazing up at the hills behind me, lingering over the last words: " 'The sun shall be turned into darkness and the moon into blood, before the great and notable day of the Lord.' The question is, my son, Is this the great and notable day of the Lord?"

I stared at him, not understanding. Then he said abruptly, "Did you ever hear speak of the prophet Jesus over in Capernaum?"

"Often," I replied. "Last year, people seemed to talk of little else; this year, I hear less. They say he has gone to Jerusalem, and those who come up from the capital say he is still doing miracles."

He nodded thoughtfully. "Then maybe it is there, at the capital, that he will establish his kingdom," he said. "Here, he refused. How gladly would we have crowned him king up there on the mountain, but he slipped away, up into the rocks, and next day the people were divided again and some had changed their minds. And yet, he fulfilled so much of what was written; when else, and at whose hand, were the eyes of the blind opened or the ears of the deaf unstopped? At whose touch did the lame man leap as a hart, or the tongue of the dumb sing? If he is the Messiah, he will establish his kingdom and the great and notable day of the Lord will dawn."

He appeared to have forgotten me and turned away. I left him with the child in his arms, chanting, trancelike, to the hills and the water.

I set off, rowing swiftly, soaking myself in the warmth and radiance of that afternoon. I felt as though I had never seen light before. I wondered how long it had lasted and wanted to get home and ask Benjamin about it. I had quite forgotten my quarrel with my aunt and when I hurried into the house, she appeared to have forgotten it too. She was making her usual preparations for the Sabbath, but I noticed that her hands were trembling and her face was very pale.

"Oh, Aunt," I cried, "are you all right? I was all alone in that terrible darkness and it seemed to last hours."

She turned and I saw naked fear in her eyes. "It lasted from the sixth hour to the ninth hour," she whispered, "and they say that it foretells some terrible disaster; so terrible, that the sun has hidden its face from us."

I did not answer, but I stood thinking. It would soon be sunset and the lake shimmered, rose and silver beneath a sky shot with crimson. The darkness had passed and the light now shone more clearly than ever before. Surely then, the disaster had already fallen. I shivered as they lit the lamp; instead of the calm peace of a Sabbath evening, everyone seemed restless and afraid.

The restlessness persisted, and the strange certainty that something had happened; women lingered at the well and men talked in low voices at street corners, or gathered around the boats. But it was five days after the Sabbath, when the first pilgrims returned from Jerusalem, that we heard the news. For they rode into Capernaum, not as happy pilgrims who have kept the feast, but silent and unwilling to talk. Nevertheless, the rumors spread of strange and terrible happenings in the capital; emergency meetings of the Sanhedrin, riots and arrests in the streets, thick darkness, and earthquake, and the veil in the temple suddenly, inexplicably, rent in two.

"And the prophet Jesus, was he there?" the question hung in the air.

The answer came like a clap of thunder.

"Oh, yes, he was there, right in the midst of it all. They crucified him."

17

I suppose one never realizes the value of a thing until one loses it, and I had certainly never realized what a hold that prophet, whom I had never seen, had on my life, until it was all over. Almost without knowing, I had come to accept all I had heard. The evidence seemed so convincing; demons, nature, sickness, blindness, and death itself had been conquered by him, and I had truly come to believe that the ultimate power in the universe, stronger than all the forces of evil, was the power that resided in him and flowed out to mankind in acts of goodness and mercy. And to believe this was to stand secure with one's feet on a rock.

But now my world had caved in and I did not want to think about it. His enemies, mere men, had conquered him after all and, in the end, he had hung weak and defenseless on a Roman cross; and he who had raised the dead had been overcome by death. He had been an impostor, after all. The ultimate power now lay with evil and chance and fate, and the world was no longer a safe place. So I blocked my mind to the whole incident, turned from the emptiness inside me, and set out to enjoy the pleasures of each day as it came. I did not wish to listen to the many stories and rumors carried by the Passover pilgrims, for I had lost interest in the man about whom they talked. The weather was hot, the harvest ripening, the lake warm and blue, and the fish abundant; also there was plenty of work to do and of this I was glad. There was no time to think during the day and, at night, I was tired and slept heavily; and sometimes my uncle took Benjamin and me in the boat, to help with the swelling nets. On such nights I would work furiously and try and forget that I had once imagined that his feet had walked the waves.

Benjamin and Joel were also speculating on the forthcoming visit to Jerusalem during the feast of Pentecost, fifty days after the Passover. This was the time when pilgrims flocked to the capital from all over the known world, and they all had to eat. My uncle went most years with dry salted fish to sell in the markets, and a very profitable expedition it was! Benjamin had been with him in the past, but now he was considered old enough and reliable enough to stay in charge of the business at home. It had been rumored, although not actually said, that Joel and I were to go this year as porters and donkey drivers, and I had been thrilled at the prospect.

It was a few days after that fateful Passover, when all Capernaum still buzzed with talk of the crucifixions in Jerusalem, that my uncle brought up the subject. Perhaps he had noticed my dull distress and wanted to give me something else to think about. We were sitting on the beach, checking the mesh after the catch, when he suddenly said; "How would you like to go to Jerusalem, Philo? You've never been south, have you? I think you and Joel could manage the donkeys and the loading and unloading this year. You've worked hard, and the trip would do you good."

He spoke kindly, no doubt expecting me to be delighted, as I would have been earlier. But I only stared at him, realizing, with a sense of shock, that I no longer wanted to go to Jerusalem.

It seemed a haunted city; I did not want to stand and look up at that hill outside the city wall where he, the healer and conqueror, had been defeated and murdered. I did not want to mingle with the crowds who had yelled for his death. I wanted to forget him and I did not even want to go home, for I had an idea that my mother and sisters would obstinately continue to believe in him against all the evidence, and I would be a mere outsider again. But I could not explain all this to my uncle, so I just said, after a pause, "As you will, Uncle; if I can be useful, I will come." I think he was disappointed, but Joel's delight made up for it, and the plans for the expedition went ahead.

Our little pickling shed had become far too small for the large spring catches, and Benjamin and I often rowed the dinghy, laden with fish, to the salting and pickling sheds at Tarichaea, returning with the last lot, ready for storing. I enjoyed these quiet journeys, and we often pulled in for a quick swim. One of our favorite beaches was the Bay of Tabgha, shaped like a small amphitheatre with lush fields rising behind it. It was usually deserted when we returned in the heat of the day, and we were therefore surprized when, drawing in one morning, we saw a boat moored and a young man, his fishing tackle folded beside him, sitting gazing out across the lake. Benjamin shaded his eyes and nearly dropped his oar in amazement.

"It's John Zebedee," he gasped. "He and his brother left their boat to follow the prophet, and all for nothing. I suppose he must have come back to his fishing. He must be feeling awful, poor chap!"

"Well, let's go on," I said hurriedly. "He won't want us, and—and, I don't really want to hear about it either."

"No," replied Benjamin firmly, "he and James were our friends, and he's seen us now. We can at least tell him we're glad he's back, I expect they are all laughing at him in the town and he'll need his friends."

I said no more for I respected the kind, loyal spirit in Benjamin and often wished I was more like him. We rowed in swiftly and jumped ashore.

"Peace be to you, John," said Benjamin rather shyly. "We are glad you are home. Will you be working with us again?"

He shook his head and smiled, and I stared at him in surprise, for there was no trace of sadness or disillusionment in that smile, no weariness in that ringing voice.

"Oh no; this, last night, was our final fishing trip. I've just been mending the net to take it back to my father. We must get back to Jerusalem as soon as possible. He told us to come up north and meet him in Galilee, but now we are needed in the capital."

There was a hint of excitement in his voice and we stood silent, uncertain of what to say next. I wondered whether grief had driven him mad. After a short pause, Benjamin said quietly, "We were sorry, John. It must have been a terrible time for you."

"Yes," replied John simply, "it was the most terrible day of my life, just as the first day of the week was the most joyful. How dull and blind we were! We never understood, although he tried so

145

hard to tell us."

We continued staring, silent and uneasy.

"You mean," went on John, "that you haven't heard? Or that you just can't believe it!" He was laughing now, and his eyes sparkled with some joyful mystery. "Sit down," he said suddenly, "and tell me what you've heard."

"We heard he was crucified," I said miserably. "But we don't hear much. Benjamin's grandfather is a rabbi. I think they wanted him dead."

"But he's not dead, he's alive! I had breakfast with him this morning." John pointed to a ring of blackened stones, enclosing ashes. "He stood on the beach at dawn and called us in and gave us hot food. He talked most to Peter, but he told us to return to Jerusalem and meet him there. As soon as I've patched the net, I'm off with the others."

The world seemed to be reeling. I wondered if I was dreaming and would wake up on my pallet on the roof. I burrowed my heels in the sand; it was real and warm and gritty.

"Then did they not really crucify him?" I asked respectfully.

"Oh yes, they crucified him. I stood by the cross and watched him for nine whole hours."

"But they let him go? I did not know that anyone ever survived crucifixion."

"He didn't; he died all right, and we buried him. But death could not hold him. He came back. He is much stronger than death; in fact, he is life. He often told us so, but we did not understand what he was talking about."

We sat rigid. Benjamin glanced at me, his brows furrowed. I think that he too feared that John had gone out of his mind, and was signaling that we had better get away. But I had seen that look in other faces, and, whether he was mad or sane, I wanted to hear this through.

"But, Master John," I pleaded, "if he is really stronger than death, why did he ever die at all? Why did he ever let the Romans touch him? After all, they overcame him and nailed him up, didn't they?"

John shook his head. "No," he said, speaking very slowly, "they never overcame him. It seemed like it at the time and I wept like the rest; but looking back—I see it differently. All the hate and the mocking and the spitting—yet they never conquered his love. He loved to the end. When they drove the nails into his hands, he asked his Father to forgive them; said they didn't know what they were doing. His love was stronger than all their hate; they couldn't overcome it."

He was gazing across the lake again, and I wondered if he had forgotten us. I touched him timidly. "But Master John," I faltered, "why, then did he let them capture him and torture him and kill him? Why? Why? He could have stopped them easily, couldn't he?"

"Oh, yes," he replied, still speaking very slowly, "he could have stopped them with a word. He said so himself. He told them that if he asked for them, his Father would send twelve legions of angels to save him; but he didn't ask. I think that, in order to defeat an enemy, you have to meet him face to face and that, in order to defeat death, the Master had to go right down into death and confront him; just as, in order to defeat cruelty and hate, his love had to confront the suffering of crucifixion; that's how it seems to me now. But I must go; the others will be ready to start."

He smiled at us and leaped to his feet; he ran to the boat, hauled the net aboard and set off toward Capernaum, rowing with swift, even strokes. Benjamin and I watched him, fascinated, and then turned to stare at the blackened stones, the ashes and the fish heads.

"Here—this morning!" said Benjamin dreamily. Then he added, "We must go too. We've got to tell them."

I did not inquire what he meant; I was far too confused and uncertain to say anything at all. We journeyed in silence, but I noticed that Benjamin rowed as for a race. We moored the boat and carried our freight up to the shed as usual, but the moment he had stacked it in place he turned and rushed into the house. I followed him.

My aunt sat in the house and Leah, her sister from Jerusalem, was with her. Leah came often, and she and my aunt would talk for hours on end. They were talking when Benjamin entered, unwashed, soiled and smelling of fish.

"Benjamin," said his mother sharply, "have you forgotten—"

He cut her off in the middle of her sentence; his eyes blazed with excitement.

"Alive!" he shouted, "alive and back from the dead! John Zebedee had breakfast with him on the beach at Tabgha this morning."

Leah drew in her breath and started forward, but my aunt's face was contorted with fear and anger and she flung up her hand, as though to ward off a blow. "It's a lie," she screamed, "and if you ever say that again I'll have your grandfather thrash you within an inch of your life. Your father's no good; you've all turned against us; you're all deceived by this wicked trickster. Leah, go home, and I never want you to come here again."

She ran out of the room, tears streaming down

her cheeks, but Leah seized Benjamin by the shoulders, her face alight with triumph.

"Of course it's true," she cried. "That's what he said to poor Martha. 'I am the Resurrection and the Life.' Can life die? Of course he's alive!"

18

I think it was at this point that I really believed; not just because he had conquered death, but because those whom he had touched seemed alive in a different way. If he was really life, victorious over death, the elements, demons and sickness, then that explained everything; the calm, purposeful joy of John Zebedee, Illyrica's peace and healing, the clear happiness of the man in Gadara. But he had never touched me and perhaps—perhaps, it was not too late. I suddenly wanted desperately to go to Jerusalem. In fact, like Joel, I could hardly wait.

But there were still some four Sabbaths to go before the Feast of Pentecost and plenty of work to be done. The weather was scorching, the hillsides brown and dry, flowerless except for the great blue thistles. Very little was said about the prophet openly, for the rumor that he was alive had been severely squashed by the Pharisees and anyone heard mentioning it was liable to severe punishment. Yet his disciples had talked and the rumor lingered, like some subtle incense. People smiled secretly and looked at each other with questioning eyes. His name was seldom heard yet ever present, and a strange sense of hidden expectancy hung over the land.

Yet times passes, however slowly, and the day came when Joel and I were sent to bed long before sundown, far too excited to sleep, yet deeply asleep when my uncle's foot prodded us awake. We rose dizzily, helped load the asses by moon and lantern light, and I ate a hearty breakfast while my aunt packed food for the journey. I said a hasty farewell to a rather wistful Benjamin and then we were off, joining many others on the southern road, along the black margin of the lake, under the setting stars. By now I was wildly excited, longing to beat the trundling asses to make them go faster, but my uncle held me back. "Just walk steadily," he said. "We want to cover as much of the plain as possible, before the noonday sun forces us to stop."

We were not going far that day; only some twenty miles to the southwest, where we would spend the night at Nazareth. We journeyed quietly, and I listened to the tapping of the donkeys' hooves on the road, our own steady footfalls, the lapping of small waves on the pebbles and it was like sweet music to my ears. We were on our way to Jerusalem.

We turned through a rift in the hills and by the time we came out on to the plain of Gennesaret, it was light and the farmers were already at work in the fields. We followed the road through the most fertile, abundant countryside that I had ever seen. Every inch seemed cultivated. Golden strips of cut grain lay side by side with plantations of date palms or vineyards, or pale green and gold gave place to silvery gray, where the olive groves began, while around the farms clustered the rich green of fig and walnut trees, making arbors of shade as the sun rose higher.

It was so still, so sheltered, that I felt we were walking, half asleep, across enchanted ground. Late reapers were still winnowing their grain, tossing it in the air and the mists of chaff, caught on the tiny breeze, added to the dreamlike atmosphere. But the people were friendly and called greetings to the pilgrims, and at about the sixth hour, when the sun beat fiercely down and Joel's feet were beginning to drag, my uncle led us off the road to the shade of an ancient mulberry tree. The owner of the tree came out, invited us to draw water from his well, offered us ripe figs and wished us peace in the name of the God of Israel. We watered the asses and led them to the shade where the unscorched grass was still thick and luscious, then my uncle produced a meal of bread, fish, cucumber, and goat cheese and we drank from the wineskin. When we had finished, Joel and I lay flat on our backs and slept.

My uncle kicked us awake when the sun's rays were slanting and the air a little cooler. We loaded the asses, drank from the well, and set off again, leaving the plain for the hill country. Well before sunset, we trotted the beasts down the parched slopes of the basin in the hills that shelter Nazareth. It stands a little way off the road, its square white houses huddled on the side of a slope, with an open market place at the entrance and the synagogue built on the crest. We were to stay with a cousin of my aunt's who had married a Nazarene farmer, and they made us very welcome. Their oldest son, Isaac, was about Joel's age; he helped us stable the beasts and then took us round the farm and the marketplace.

The market square was a quiet place compared with Capernaum. Most of the men had shut their stalls and gone up to the synagogue for evening worship, but a few of the shops were still open. We stopped in front of the carpenter's shop and watched him hack away at an ill-fitting yoke, while the ox stood by. The beast had a bleeding sore on his shoulder and Isaac, a true farmer's son, touched him gently.

"It was never like this when Jesus kept the shop," he said sadly. "He fitted the yokes so carefully. But he'll never come back; they've crucified him."

I turned on him. "You don't mean the prophet, do you?" I gasped. "You don't mean to say—You must mean someone else!"

Isaac turned away, perhaps because there were tears in his eyes.

"I don't know whether he was a prophet or not," he said dully. "People here in the town say that he was mad, but he was a wonderful carpenter. He used to make things for us and mend our toys. All the children loved him. But that was a long time ago. He's only been back once in the last three years—and now—"

His voice trailed off sorrowfully. Joel had lingered to watch a potter, but I stood rigid. It must be the same; crucifixions were not common just then, and neither were prophets. But I had never known that he had worked as a craftsman; it seemed to put him in a new light and to bring him nearer. Then the door of Isaac's home opened and his mother called across the square, to tell us that supper was ready, so we hurried over, washed our hands and joined the group reclining round the big clay dish, on which was served a boiled chicken with lentils and vegetables, followed by figs and dates. It was a friendly meal, and our host's old father joined us. But apart from blessing the food, he said very little and, like Isaac, he seemed sad.

"What has Isaac been showing you out there?" asked the farmer, as we leaned back after our meal.

"Has he shown you our camels?"

I nodded. There was only one subject I really wanted to talk about, and it wasn't camels.

"We stopped at the carpenter's shop and watched him fit a yoke," I said. "Isaac told us that the prophet Jesus used to work here, in Nazareth, as a carpenter."

The family glanced uneasily at the old man, but he looked up as I spoke and joined in the conversation for the first time.

"Ah, things are not now like they were then," he said mournfully, stroking his long white beard. "They came to him from all over the district in those days. His yokes lay so easy, the beasts never knew they were wearing them and the furniture he made would outlast a woman's lifetime; never bothered much about money either. His father, Joseph, was my friend; he was a good carpenter, but his son was better. When he took over the business—"

The old man stopped to sip his wine. He was well away now and we leaned back and listened respectfully as he rambled on.

"Did they always live here?" asked my uncle.

"Joseph and I grew up together as lads, and I knew Mary as a little lass. I remember their betrothal. Then, something went wrong. Joseph never told me, but there was a lot of talk about Mary. He took her south to register in the city of his ancestors and they never returned for about five years. Then they came back with a little boy. He was a wonderful scholar; the rabbi thought he would make a scribe of him, but he took over the family business—best carpenter in Galilee— I loved him as my own son—but he left the shop to his brothers and went away—"

The old man trailed off and looked round

pitifully. Nobody spoke.

"He came back once," he went on, "but they all turned against him. They tried to kill him, but they couldn't. You were there, Amos; why did they try to kill him? I could never understand it."

"He claimed to be the Lord's Messiah," said Amos reverently, "but we knew that our carpenter could not be *he*. They said he had done great miracles, but he did none here, except just at the end. The scribes and rulers of the synagogue said he had blasphemed and must die. They dragged him to the top of the cliff to throw him over and I went along with the crowd to see if I could persuade them to free him, because, after all, he was my friend and I thought he had lost his reason. But he didn't need my help. Just as they seized him to fling him over, he turned and walked back down the hill. He didn't even run! They were shouting and clawing at him, but he didn't seem to see them; just walked home and no one could touch him. There's a miracle for you, if you like!"

Amos chuckled, but the old grandfather leaned forward, deeply distressed.

"You said they couldn't kill him," he cried. But the old men in the market say that the Romans crucified him. It's not true, is it? They couldn't kill him, here or there, could they?"

No one spoke. Joel opened his mouth, but my uncle kicked him and I gave him a warning look.

"Don't believe all you hear, Father," said his daughter-in-law comfortingly. "There are lots of rumors about. Now we will spread out the sleeping mats. Philo and Joel, you can go up on the roof with Isaac. Martha, clear away the supper and sweep the room."

My uncle, our host and Isaac had gone outside to look at the beasts; his wife and Martha were clearing the room. I looked around for Joel. He had slipped into the corner and was sitting close to the old man. He was saying something and the grandfather was leaning sideways, cupping his ear to hear. The oil lamp flickered in the draught, lighting up their faces, the one, bright-eyed and eager, the other so deeply wrinkled and unhappy. I drew nearer to listen.

"Don't be troubled, Master Reuben," whispered Joel. "He's alive; our neighbor, John Zebedee, had breakfast with him."

A look of infinite peace and relief swept over the old man's face. "The child speaks the truth," he murmured. "I knew it. They could not kill him, either here or there. He is alive."

We were awakened next morning by the cocks crowing from the farms, and we were soon on the road after a quick breakfast and a hasty farewell. But we all paused for a moment on the hill leading down from Nazareth, and gazed out over the Plain of Esdraelon stretching away, like a fertile oasis toward the brown mountains of Samaria. It still lay in shadow but, to the right, the long ridge of Mount Carmel caught the brightness that burned behind Tabor. Joel, wide awake by now, and much enjoying himself, beguiled the way by telling us stories, learned from the scrolls at the synagogue, about the places on our route; thrilling tales of old Hebrew heroes who had fought on the plain or in the Valley of Jezreel, or of King Saul who had died on Mount Gilboa, just above us. The great invading armies of Assyria, Babylon, Persia, and Greece had marched across this plain and my uncle listened too, smiling to himself, for he had never studied the scrolls and knew little of Israel's history.

More and more pilgrims joined us on the road,

some singing psalms or reciting prayers as they traveled, so it was not a dull journey. Once again, we rested at noon and in the evening we came to the old city of Beth Shan. "But it is not Beth Shan any longer," Joel informed us. "The Greeks have rebuilt it and called it Scythopolis. Let's get to the Hebrew quarter quickly and settle the asses, and get away from all these statues."

I hurried along with him, realizing that, for a Jewish boy, the statues were a defilement and a breach of his holy law, but I thought they were beautiful. Later, I wandered alone along the fine pavements, looking up at the marble temples built to the various gods of Greece, and rejoiced to hear my mother's native tongue spoken freely. What amazing skill and craftsmanship had gone into the building of those temples! And these gods, who were they? Had they ever come down to men and healed the sick, or cast out demons or raised the dead? No, as far as I knew, they sat apart in their temples and there was no meeting place. But my prophet (I had nearly said my God) had worked as a carpenter and had fitted easy yokes on the backs of tired oxen. I turned back thoughtfully to the inn, where we were to sleep, and said nothing about the beauties of the city.

On the third day we tramped along the crowded highway, with the stark, treeless mountains of Gilead and Ephraim rising on either side. That night we camped under the stars and woke to find our cloaks drenched with dew. It was a sweltering day, and as we dropped further and deeper below sea level, I felt as though I was descending into an airless pit; a weird, dead-looking world of sandy rock, twisted into grotesque shapes by ancient earthquakes. Our young legs were getting used to long marches but, all the same, we were thoroughly glad to see, in the late afternoon, a great oasis of green ahead of us and to know that we were approaching Jericho, the city of palm trees.

We passed into the crowded streets, and stared around in amazement, for this was a city built by the late King Herod in modern Roman style, with his own dazzling white palace to the southwest of it. But we were too tired and hot to see much, and almost fought our way to the inn, for here we were meeting up with streams of pilgrims from across the Jordan. We unloaded and watered the donkeys with what seemed the last ounce of our strength, ate our supper, and lay down, but this time I could not sleep. The air was stuffy under the low, straw roof and thick with the smell of sweating humanity. Joel dropped off immediately but, after a time, I got up and joined my uncle, who sat out in the moonlight with a group of travelers. The innkeeper had joined them and they were all talking earnestly.

"This feast will not be like other feasts," said the innkeeper quietly. "The Romans are afraid and their spies are everywhere. No one dares speak openly. It was an evil day when they crucified that prophet, and they haven't got rid of him yet. Rumors are everywhere, and they can't quell them. Something very strange is happening in Jerusalem, but no one quite knows what it is."

There was a troubled murmur of assent, and my uncle said, "Did the prophet ever come to this city?"

"Oh yes." The innkeeper must have told the story many times, but he seemed eager to tell it again. "He could have been very popular; all the best people were waiting to receive him and to see miracles, but he made a big mistake; he went to stay with the scum of the city—a little tax-gatherer who, through bribery and corruption, had managed to make himself one of the richest men in the town."

"And the prophet stayed with him? Why should he do that?"

"Nobody knows. Nobody wanted Zacchaeus in the crowd at all. They hated him. But he climbed a tree and the prophet passed right under it. You would have thought it had all been planned. He stopped and looked up and told the little wretch to come down; said he was coming to stay with him. The people in the crowd were furious; some of them had hoped the prophet would stay with them. But no! Off he goes to Zacchaeus's mansion. But, the funny part is, that's not the end of the story."

"What happened?"

"The prophet went back to Jerusalem, and you'll never believe what happened next."

"Tell us."

"Zacchaeus goes trotting around the town, knocking at the doors. No one wants to open at first; they all think he's after their money, but he's not. He's chasing all the people he robbed and giving them back four times as much as he took, and as for the poor and the beggars, he's given them about half his property, and if you don't believe me, I don't blame you."

The innkeeper chuckled, but our faces were sober. Who was this man, who so changed people's actions and personalities, who could bring such good out of evil? And why had they crucified him? The unspoken question hung in the air.

"Did he do any miracles here?" asked one pilgrim.

"Oh yes, just as he was leaving, he healed a

blind beggar, right at the city gate. The man rose up and followed the prophet on to Jerusalem. He's there now and it's the same with all those who had anything to do with the prophet. They are all up in Jerusalem, waiting for something to happen."

A small breeze fanned my forehead, and my eyes suddenly felt heavy. I crept away and lay down. Tomorrow we would travel the last twenty-five miles to Jerusalem, and I would be waiting for something to happen. I had no idea what.

19

The road from Jericho to Jerusalem is, I suppose, one of the hottest and dryest in the world. We left before daybreak, but even so the air was heavy, and we sweated as we walked. In the half light, the twisted rocks and barren landscape emerged weird and ghostly, and we kept well together, for this desolate territory was the well-known hiding place of thieves and cut-throats, and many travelers had been robbed and left to die. We stopped, before noon, at the inn by the roadside and rested for some hours and, when we started again, we were conscious of a freshening of the atmosphere and we breathed more deeply as we climbed. Pilgrims smiled at each other, for they were approaching the climax of their journey, the heights of Mount Zion. And when we turned the corner of the Mount of Olives, and saw the Holy City with its shining temple bright against a western sky, many wept for joy and some knelt to worship. The pilgrims journeyed the last lap singing praises and psalms to the God of Israel.

We lodged in a house in the south of the city; it had a small upper guest room and a courtyard where the asses could lie. The coolness of the higher air was like a tonic, and we all felt refreshed. The owner of the house was one of my aunt's large, scattered family, and he and his wife made quite a fuss of Joel, whom they had never seen before. They prepared an appetizing meal for us and we were ready to sleep early after the heat and weariness of the journey. When we woke next morning, Naomi, the lady of the house, told us that my uncle had gone to meet the fishmongers' guild and we were free to do as we liked until the midday meal.

Joel looked straight up at her. "I want to see the place where the Romans crucify people," he demanded.

She looked startled and shocked but then shrugged her shoulders. "Oh well," she said, "you're a man now, aren't you, so I suppose you can see what you want. Golgotha lies outside the city wall, near the northwest corner. But there are better things than that to see in Jerusalem."

We left the house, Joel leading the way. I was surprized too, and unwilling to follow. "Why don't we go and look at the temple?" I asked rather crossly. "There won't by anything to see up there; they'll have taken down the beams long ago."

He turned on me, quivering with eagerness.

"Don't you see, Philo?" he pleaded. "If he's alive, we've got to find him. Nobody seems to know that he's alive, and you and Father won't let me tell them. He must be somewhere, and if we go to the places where people saw him and know about him, we're bound to hear something."

There seemed some sense in that, so we set off to climb Mount Zion on the northwest, where the rich mansions rose behind high walls surrounded by watered gardens, and Herod's great, glittering palace lay to our left. We passed through the city gate and there, just outside the wall, we came to our journey's end. The little hill rose steeply, and it was easy to see why it was called the place of a skull, for the shadowed hollows of the rocks resembled eye sockets with other rocks protruding between them. It was only too easy to imagine the three gibbets, the screaming crowd, the nailed, twisted forms; I turned away with a shudder, only to find an old beggar at my side, watching us closely. He was a filthy old man, but his eyes were bright and intelligent, and he knew what we were looking at.

"That's the place, young master," he whispered. "That's where they strung them up; two murderers and a madman. You should have seen the crowds! Could you spare a coin for a poor beggar, sir?"

I had no money and would have pushed him aside in disgust, but Joel stepped across. "Where did they bury him?" he asked.

"They buried the murderers down at the foot of their crosses," said the old man, looking round furtively to see that no one was listening, "but the madman—he must have been somebody! A nobleman and a Pharisee came and took away his body and they say that the nobleman buried it in his own tomb; down there, in the garden by the city wall."

Quite near to us stood an enclosed garden with a gate guarded by a Roman soldier. He seemed to be watching us closely and I dared not linger to look through the bars, I was suddenly overcome by a terrible feeling of hopelessness and futility and all my doubts came surging back. Why were we searching for this crucified man, who was either dead or had gone into hiding, and what had he achieved, and where was the kingdom of which he had spoken? All around me beggars whined, merchants haggled and cheated, the rich oppressed the poor, and Roman soldiers, cruel and arrogant, strutted in the streets. For all the fine talk, he had made no difference, left no impression, and besides, I was hungry.

"Come home," I said to Joel. "There's nothing here, and it's time for dinner. Hurry, or we shall be late."

Joel followed me quietly enough, but he was more determined than I had realized. As soon as we were all gathered round the earthenware dish, he started again.

"Mistress Naomi," he began, "did you ever see that prophet whom the Romans crucified?"

There was a moment's silence and I caught that faint nervous flicker in the eyes of husband and wife as they glanced at each other; but our host answered calmly enough.

"Oh yes, I saw him when he rode in at the Golden Gate on an ass's colt. The people mistook him for their Messiah and they all began shouting and throwing palm branches. I think we all wondered—But only a week later, they were shouting for his death and he was arrested. So we made a mistake, and that's all there is to it."

"But perhaps he was their Messiah," insisted Joel.

Another moment of tense silence and again, that breathless flicker of fear; but this time, my uncle intervened. "That's enough, Joel," he said rather sharply. "I'm not too clear about this Messiah, but if it had been he, they would not have crucified him. Now, get on with your dinner."

Still no one spoke, until Naomi changed the subject. There was no more talk of the prophet until that night, when I went up to the room on the roof and found Joel leaning on the parapet, gazing out over the Kedron Valley toward the Mount of Olives.

"They say he was arrested over there, in a garden," said Joel, as though the conversation had never left off. "If we went over there and found the garden, someone might tell us something."

"I don't suppose anyone would tell us anything," I replied gloomily, "and anyhow, how do you know that he was arrested in that garden?"

"Oh, I talk to people," said Joel vaguely. "And, at Golgotha, the beggar knew. Everyone knows, but they are afraid to talk about it. Philo, we've got to find him."

But I was disappointed and sleepy and thoroughly depressed.

"You'll get yourself into a lot of trouble, if you talk about it all the time," I snapped. "And you can't do anything tomorrow; we've got to sell fish in the market all day. That's what you came for, don't forget."

Next day was a busy, profitable day for although much of our load had been sold to fish merchants, there was still some to be peddled in the market. My uncle erected a small booth and took the money, while Joel and I strung the dried fish on to reeds and handed them to the customers. Trade was brisk, and there was little time to look around, but, now and again, there was a lull and I could gape for a few moments at the amazing scenes in the lower market. Jews, or Jewish converts, from all over the known world, seemed to have gathered, and other nationalities, who had come to see the sights of Jerusalem, thronged the streets. Many different languages were being spoken in the marketplace that morning, and I saw many dark faces and strange costumes. The hours passed swiftly and, toward the end of the day, having sold our stock, Joel and I were sent off to water the beasts.

"I watched all day, but he wasn't there," said Joel suddenly, over the back of his donkey.

"Would you recognize him, if you saw him in all that crowd?"

"Oh yes; you couldn't forget him. He dressed like everyone else, but he was quite different."

"How?"

"I don't know; I can't explain. People just wanted to get near him."

I gave it up. In any case, in the confusion of those vast crowds, I had given up all hope of finding him; and, away from Benjamin and the quiet spaces of the lake, I had begun to wonder if the whole thing had been, after all, a huge hoax.

We were up early on the day of the feast. Joel, as the son of a Jewess, was to go with his cousins to the temple. The cousins owned land on the outskirts of the city and the special loaves, made from the new grain, were ready baked. They would enter the outer court and go on through the Beautiful Gate that led to the inner court, but I was only allowed in the court of the Gentiles. My uncle, who had seen it all many times before, had gone off to visit a friend in the fish industry.

So I was alone, pushing my way through the great crowds that thronged toward the temple and I was enjoying myself. The feast of Pentecost was not, like the Passover, a very solemn affair. It celebrated the gathering in of the barley harvest and, until the grapes ripened, the country people had some time to spare and a little money in their pockets. Booths lined the streets, decorated with summer garden flowers and there was a general air of gaiety and enjoyment. It was about the third hour of the day and the sun, rising over the Mount of Olives, had reached the city so that the little streets between the shops were striped with light and shade. The noise of the throng, and the lowing of animals to be sacrificed, was almost deafening, and yet we were all suddenly conscious of a strange roaring sound, like a mighty wind.

It had to be heard; people stood arrested in the streets and even the animals seemed quiet for a few moments. Then everyone turned in one direction, fear stamped on their faces, for the great disturbance of the elements seemed to have gathered force and to be whirling over one part of the city, and, in another moment, everyone was pressing in one direction.

I was simply carried with them, as helpless as a leaf on the current of the river. Yet, being a tall lad, I could see where we were going and, by good chance, I was well to the front when we seemed to gather round a large house with an upper room, over which the strange rush of air still whirlpooled. As we passed, the door in the roof room opened and a crowd of people surged down the outer staircase, singing and praising God as the pilgrims had done, some in a language I had never heard before, but with a look on their faces that I recognized. It was unmistakable; they might have been there, among this crowd, for this was where they belonged; my sister, Illyrica, the man from Gadara, Mary and little Astarte, whose eyes were opened. There must have been more than a hundred of them, pouring out into the street like the glad heralds of some new era. "He has come back to us," they cried. "He has fulfilled his promise."

The gaping throng was stirred. Something very strange was happening. Even the many strangers, men from Egypt and Mesopotamia, and Arab camel drivers, were pressing forward as though they understood. Everyone seemed to understand

and to marvel. What was happening? Who had come?

"They're drunk!" shouted someone, and a few of the coarser spirits laughed uproariously. But at the sound of their mirth one, who seemed to be the leader, mounted the stairs and motioned for silence. Eleven others stood on the stairway just below him and, to my amazement, I recognized John Zebedee among them. Then I forgot everything except the speaker, for his rough coat and thick accent were blessedly familiar. He was a Galilean and, as his voice rang out over the sparkling morning air, the laughter ceased and a hush fell on the crowd.

"We are not drunk," cried the speaker. "No one gets drunk at this hour of the morning."

People nodded; the man was talking sense.

"Don't you remember Joel's prophecy, about the signs and wonders in the last day?" continued the Galilean, and as the grand old words rolled from his lips, an uneasy ripple of fear seemed to pass over the crowd. What was coming next?

"Men of Israel, hear these words; Jesus of Nazareth—" The forbidden name fell like a thunderbolt. Was the man mad to pronounce that name, with the Roman soldiers surging up on all sides to see what was going on? Had not great bribes been given to silence anyone who knew anything about him? Of course, no one could stop the rumors, but to mention him in public!

But no one could stop the Galilean either. The news of Jesus seemed to be bursting out of him, like a cataract unloosed. On he went, working up to his final climax. "Crucified—raised up—by the right hand of God exalted—let all the house of Israel know assuredly, that God has made that same Jesus, whom you crucified, both Lord and

Christ."

There was a silence like death. Even the Roman soldiers stood rooted to the spot, and, not till years later when I studied the Hebrew scriptures, did I understand the anguish of that recognition. For centuries past, the Jews had waited and watched for their Messiah, the promised deliverer whom God would send, and suddenly in a flash, they realized what had happened and they saw their doom. The Messiah had come, and they had crucified him, and now, having defeated death, he had gone back to the God who had sent him. They had missed their great opportunity; it was all over; they were left, a people accursed. And a great cry rose up from their broken hearts, "Whatever shall we do?"

Once again, the voice of the Galilean rang out above their bowed heads and distraught faces: "Repent; be baptized in the name of Jesus for the remission of your sins; and ye shall receive the Holy Spirit."

So it was not all over; God was going to give them a second opportunity. He was coming again to his chosen race, not in the flesh, in the man they had crucified, but through his Holy Spirit. They lifted their faces, like men condemned to death who hear of a reprieve. They surged toward him and the rugged Galilean leaned toward them, pouring out his message.

And I? I turned around, seeing nothing, and somehow shouldered my way out of the crowd. I did not know or care where I was going. I just stumbled on and on. The air was growing hotter and I went out through a gate and down into a valley. The sun beat on my head and I wanted shade. I looked up and saw the terraced wall of the Mount of Olives rising ahead of me and I climbed a stony track and came to a watered garden where olive trees grew. The grass was cool and green here and the silver shade deep. I sunk down on the ground and rested my aching head.

"Men of Israel—Jesus Christ." So he had risen again and conquered death and he was not lost. He was returning to his own people, to those who had waited for their Messiah. He was victor over demons and sickness and death and would come back to them, establish his kingdom within them, and they would know him as that happy crowd had known him.

But I, the Gentile dog, would never know him, and all I had once hoped and dreamed seemed to dwindle. When I had heard that he had worked as a carpenter, I had been surprised, but not shaken. There were carpenters in Syro-Phoenicia and there were tired beasts, homes that needed furnishing, children with broken toys the world over. But, as Messiah to the Jews, he seemed a much smaller person, limited in his power and love to one little race.

And yet, he had touched Illyrica and the Gadarene and Astarte and I wondered why. I supposed he had just reached out for a moment in mercy, and then gone back to his own circle.

I supposed that it might be possible to undergo the rites of the law and to become a Jew, but I turned down that idea. He had come to the seed of David; also, on the whole, I disliked the Jews. They struck me as proud, scornful and finnicky about details; and they called me a dog.

I buried my face in my arms and wept bitterly.

20

Joel arrived home with the cousins, thrilled and shining-eyed. The cousins had always wondered about Jesus and mourned his crucifixion, but they had been too frightened to voice their thoughts. Now, they were convinced, and so was Joel and so, it seemed, were thousands of others. Rich men all over Jerusalem were opening their gardens and believers by the hundred were being baptized in their pools. Joel and the cousins had been baptized by John Zebedee, who had recognized his young neighbor.

"He and James lived just down the street," said Joel, as we lay on our mats together that night. "They used to fish alongside Father and they often came to our house, so I asked him to baptize me."

"But what for?" I asked rather crossly.

"It's a sign," said Joel, "and Jesus told us to do it. It's to show every one that my sins have been forgiven and that I'm going to start a new, clean life."

"But did you have a lot of sins?"

"Sometimes, when I sold fish in the market, I used to take some coins and buy honeycakes and lie to Father about the price. I told him about it tonight and he's forgiven me. I'm never going to do it again."

I smiled in the dark. Joel's grandfather would have thrashed him till the switch broke, on such an admission, but I did not suppose that my easy-going uncle would take a few honey cakes too seriously.

"And did you receive the Holy Spirit that they talked about?"

Joe nodded, rather shyly.

"How do you know?"

"I just didn't ever want to lie or steal again; I hated it, and felt very sad because I'd done it. Then I was very, very happy and I wanted to start again. Philo, I wish you were a Jew."

"No thanks," I replied rather bitterly, "I'm quite all right as I am. But just tell me one thing more; if he's your Messiah, and all that wonderful, why did he let the Romans crucify him?"

Joel hesitated. "Peter and John told us about that," he said slowly, "but I don't quite understand that part yet. He said it was like the last of all the sacrifices. He said Jesus offered himself as the great sacrifice for the sins of the world."

"You mean, the sins of the Jews?"

"No, that's not what he said. He said, the sins of the world."

I shrugged and turned my back on him, although I'm sure he would have gone on talking till morning. I thought I would lie awake half the night, but I fell asleep almost at once and I dreamed of home. I seemed to see my mother and sisters standing together at the door of the house, their faces flushed and tanned from the sun in the gleaning fields. They were beckoning me to come, and they seemed to have some happy secret to tell me. I wanted to run to them but my legs were heavy as lead and I awoke, sweating and struggling, as though from a nightmare. It was very early morning. I sat up and looked out east, to where the sun cast a halo of brightness behind

172

the Mount of Olives, and I knew quite clearly what I was going to do.

I lay quietly thinking until my uncle, who slept in the upper room with us, rose from his bed and went downstairs. I knew he would go straight to the yard to wash and from there, to the beasts. I waited a few minutes, then crept after him. He was examining a donkey's hoof, but he looked up and bade me good morning.

"Uncle," I said, "I want to go home as soon as possible. Of course, I'll help you back with the asses but then, please may I go?"

"But we shan't be leaving for a few days. A friend in the town wants me to stay and talk business, and Joel is pleading to be allowed to go with the cousins and hear more of the new teaching. He certainly seems a new lad. If it teaches him to be honest and brave, I've got nothing against it. In fact, it seems to me a lot better than this endless washing of hands and tithing little bits of parsley. But I don't know what his mother and grandfather are going to say."

He seemed to be considering and perhaps the thought of his wife prompted his next speech. Now that the trip to Jerusalem was over, I knew that they would not need three boys in the trade and I knew, too, that my aunt was getting increasingly critical of my presence in the house.

"I think you are right, lad," he said. "You ought to be seeing how they are getting on, and there is no need to wait. The donkeys will travel home with empty packs, so Joel and I can manage. You can go today, if you like. There will be pilgrims traveling to the coast and to the north and you can travel with them. Your best road will be up through Samaria."

This was all very sudden, but I was not really

sorry. We were parting on good terms, and I had lost all interest in Jerusalem. My uncle told me I had worked well and gave me money for the journey and a gift for my mother. "And don't spend it on honey cakes," he added with a grin.

The sunlight was already traveling down Mount Scorpus westward, dazzling on the roof of the temple. It was going to be a scorching day, and there was no time to lose. I ate a hasty meal, tied my water bottle, my cloak, and a parcel of food on my shoulder, took my staff in my hand, and set off. My uncle and Joel climbed with me to the top of the town and we said good-bye at the Damascus Gate on the northern highway. I was going home.

I dipped from the breezes of Mount Zion into the swimming air of the valleys. The road wound up and down across the low mountains of Judea and every little hill carried a village on its crest. After the excitement and rumors of Pentecost, few people were leaving the capital so soon and most Jews traveling north preferred to go home by way of Jericho, so, although I fell in with a caravan, it was only a small one. We spent the night at an inn and were away before daybreak, and crossed the border into Samaria on the second day.

We rested at noon and by early evening we stopped to drink and water the beasts at Jacob's well, not far from the village of Sychar. It was impossible to hurry in such heat although most of the pilgrims were eager to get through Samaria as quickly as possible, and hastened on to camp out of doors that night. But I lingered behind to enjoy a long, cool drink and to rest a little longer. If I waited for a time, another caravan would probably turn up.

I let down my water bottle on a string but I could not reach the water. I was wondering what to do, when a voice behind me said, "The well is deep. Do you want a pot to draw with?"

A pleasant looking boy, of about my own age, was passing with a few sheep following behind him. He was going home to Sychar. He went to a thorny bush and drew out a clay pot on a long cord. "My mother keeps that there for thirsty travelers," he explained, letting it down expertly. "Are you traveling home from Jerusalem?"

"Yes," I said. "I work for a Galilean who took fish down to sell at the feast. Now I'm on my way back to Tyre. Is there an inn at Sychar?"

He looked surprised. "Are you not a Jew then?"

"No, I'm a Syro-Phoenician."

"I thought so. No Jew would turn aside here. They hate us. They'd rather sleep out in the rain. But you don't need an inn; my mother will give you a bed in our home. She's always glad to hear news from Jerusalem."

I picked up my pack and followed him gratefully, across the level fields of faded grass to the mud town, that lay near the foot of rocky Mount Gerizim, the sacred mountain where the Samaritans worshiped. We came to a house on the outskirts and the boy pushed open the door. He and the animals entered, and the sheep lay down in the lower part of the room, waiting to be milked.

"I've brought a traveler home, Mother," said the boy. "May he stay the night and go on his way tomorrow?"

"He is welcome in the name of the Lord," said the woman. "The supper is nearly ready."

I looked at her. I was a growing lad and I recognized her beauty at once; but it was a worn, faded beauty, which had only survived in her slender figure, her tranquil eyes, and the peace that stamped her face. There appeared to be no man in the family; the son tended the sheep and watered the vines at the back of the house and the woman brought water for my hands and feet. Then we gathered round a simple meal of pulse, bread and apricots and, no sooner had we started, than she asked the same question as her boy, "Tell me, what is the latest news from Jerusalem?"

I wondered how much she knew, and hesitated, but she came to the point simply and directly. "The Christ; the Messiah, whom they crucified; they say he rose again. Has anyone seen him? Is there any further news of him?"

I stared at her, surprised. She, a Samaritan, was the first person I had met who had called him by that name with any certainty. There was nothing to hide anymore. I told her all I knew, from the meeting with John Zebedee by the lakeside, to the amazing occurrences at the feast; and, as she listened, her face seemed to grow young again with joy and wonder.

"So he has truly come back," she murmured. "I knew it; we all knew it. He was the source of the living water. Death could not hold him. Now the steams will flow out to the whole world."

I did not understand what she was talking about, but I caught the last phrase.

"Not to the world," I said, rather bitterly, "only to the Jew. He's their Messiah, you know. That's why I'm going home. I thought—oh, I don't know what I thought, but there's nothing to wait for now."

She laughed, and the sound was pure joy.

"Only to the Jew?" she said. "No, no, lad, that can't be true. It was to me, a Samaritan, that he came; to me, a sinful woman, he talked about living water. He walked all the way from Jerusalem, just to find me."

I continued staring. "Then you've seen him?"

"Seen him? He stayed here two days, in a Samaritan village. His poor disciples didn't know where to put themselves." She laughed again, and then became grave.

"I don't know whether I should tell a boy, like you, of my life of shame, but if it will help you to believe, then I will do so. My parents died when I was a child and I grew up working where I could. I was very beautiful and it was my undoing."

It was getting dark and her face was in shadow. Her son went out, and we were alone.

"Men are very cruel. One after another, they took me, used me, left me. I longed for love and care, but they never gave me that. After all, I was only a servant girl. Early on, I bore a child, the lad who is with me now. The people in the village would have stoned me, according to the law of Moses, but at that point I was in the care of a rich, influential man and he protected me and my baby. But I was an outcast, a sinner, and the loneliness was like hell. I shunned them, and they shunned me. I went to the well alone in the heat of the day to avoid them, and it was there that I met him."

"The prophet?"

"The Christ; the Messiah, the Savior of the world. I met his disciples, going to the village to buy food and they looked away, but he was sitting on the well, tired and thirsty, and he asked me for a drink. I was amazed. Then he told me about living waters, springing up into everlasting life; he told me I need never thirst again."

"What did he mean?"

"I wasn't sure; but, whatever it was, I wanted

it. Then he told me to fetch my husband. I pretended to be a widow, but he knew every detail of my spoiled, stained life. He held it up in front of me, like a picture, all the things I'd lied about and hidden. He knew them all, yet he loved me."

"How did he know?"

"He is God, the All-Knowing. I tried to change the subject, and talk about what all Jews and Samaritans argue about; is the real center of worship Mount Gerizim or Jerusalem? But he didn't seem to think it mattered much where you worship; it's how you worship that is so important. He said the time was coming when there would be no fixed place of worship, but people with clean, truthful hearts worshiping him everywhere. You couldn't change the subject with him. He brought it back to my sin."

"What did you do?"

"I asked him about the Messiah, and he said he was the Messiah. I believed him, too. I ran back to the town. I, who had skulked and hidden away with my shame and loneliness for years, was standing in the street begging them all to come and see a man who knew the worst about me, yet who loved me. They came flocking to the well. They asked him to stay, and I think nearly everybody in the village believed in him. Not being Jews, they weren't so interested in him being the Messiah. They realized he was more than that. He's the Savior of the world."

I gaped at her, only half understanding.

"He gave me the living water, but I had to put things right first, and turn my back on the old sinful life. I live here quietly with my boy, but all the hate and loneliness are gone and all the thirst is quenched. I think that the living water and the Holy Spirit of whom you speak, are one, and I believe that, one day, the streams will flow out to the whole world. But you must look at your sin with him first, and turn from it. He will not pour his clean water into a dirty vessel."

The boy came back, and we unrolled our mats. Sleep came quickly, and I woke early for I wanted to reach the borders of Samaria before the great heat of the day. My hostess gave me food for the journey and blessed me, and I set off on the northern road with much to think about. It was still dark, but the morning star hung in the sky, and the light would soon dawn behind the hills. And light was beginning to break in my spirit too; small shafts of light that did not entirely dispel the darkness but which, like the morning star, heralded some future daybreak.

"The sins of the world," Joel had said. "Men with clean, truthful hearts worshiping everywhere," the woman had said. "The Savior of the world; he came all the way to Samaria to find me—one day the rivers will flow out to the whole world—but first, you must look at your sin."

Could it be that it was not my nationality that cut me off from him, but my sin?

21

I reached home late on the fifth night of my journey. It was only two days to the new moon and very dark, but although I could see nothing except the white road ahead, I smelled the blessed salt freshness blown across the stubble fields when I was still a long way off and I quickened my steps. I was not afraid to go home. If anyone had suspected me or questioned my mother, she would have found some way to send me a message.

The house was quiet and the family asleep, but they rose up, startled at my knocking, and when they heard my voice they ran joyfully to the door and drew me in. They gave me a great welcome, which was more than I deserved, and Illyrica brought me water and my mother blew up the dead ashes and prepared food. Nothing had changed, and I realized how deeply I had missed my home. The light from the oil lamp and the burning wood flickered on my two sisters, their dark hair dishevelled, their faces rosy with sleep; Illyrica, a little shy and withdrawn, Ione, completely self-forgetful in her joy. Whatever the problems ahead, I was very glad to be back.

My mother reappeared with flat loaves, fried eggs, and a cruse of sheep's milk and I ate my fill. We talked for a time, but we spoke of nothing important, just family news and local events. But

I knew there was more to come, for, now and again, my mother and Illyrica would glance at each other and my sister would lower her eyes and smile. Well, I was willing to wait. I, too, was not ready to speak about Pentecost, nor the crucifixion.

But, next morning, when my sisters had gone to the well, my mother poured out the real news. She went to a corner of the room, drew out a lump of mud and plaster from the wall, and produced a large packet.

"What is that, Mother?" I asked.

"I'll tell you." She settled herself and smiled mysteriously. "Philo, Illyrica is betrothed."

"I'm not surprised; she's very beautiful. Who is he?"

"He's a very rich man, Philo, the younger brother of Mistress Cyrene whose husband was a leper. She has never forgotten how Ione brought that about and, as you know, she treats the child as her daughter, and is always sending for her to help with the little boy or to do some household tasks. We have never been really needy since her husband was cured, although the girls were gleaning for a time. Anyhow, Illyrica went up to the house with a message about the wool we prepare (they send us fleece from their sheep) and Ione, who has never learned to behave properly, dragged her inside. They were playing together with the child when he came out and saw her."

"Did he speak to her?"

"Oh no, he is a very good-mannered young man. He asked his sister about her and, in spite of our lowly station, she praised Illyrica highly. It was love at first sight, and the first I knew about it was when I was summoned to the great house. Mistress Cyrene talked to me a little and then the young man asked me for Illyrica's hand, and he offered such a bride price, that it took my breath away. But then, he is very rich and he owns much land. You should see the jewels and raiment he has bought her. They are up at Mistress Cyrene's house, and he will take her as soon as the grape and olive harvests are over."

"And was Illyrica willing?"

"Oh yes; she is sixteen now and should have married long ago. She has not seen him since that first day, but she knows the family and he is well spoken of in the town. He will make her a good husband and she will live near to us."

"I'm glad. What about the bride price?"

My mother fingered the packet in her lap and was silent. I waited.

"Philo," she said, looking up at last, "I lied to you about your father's boat. There was no money left. He gave me a mean price, but I was at his mercy. I gave it all to the soothsayer."

It was my turn to say nothing; I had gone off leaving them in utter poverty. My cheeks burned with shame.

"But, Philo, I can make it up to you now. I have saved the bride price. You can buy back your father's boat."

"Hiram would never sell it," I gasped.

"I'm not so sure. You haven't heard what happened. Two of his ships were burned the night you went away."

"Two?" I echoed, looking up.

"Yes, two." There was a faint smile on my mother's lips and I realized that she had not questioned me about my reason for running away. "The flames from the first were so fierce, that they caught the second and scorched everything around. Only your father's boat was spared."

So that accounts for my cloak, I thought, but aloud I said, "Well, why should he want to sell that now?"

"I haven't finished. He is an evil man, and his crew hate him. One morning, about a month ago, there was a fight in the market. They said he had cheated them of their wages and he was beaten up. That night, not one of the crew turned up. He hired a couple of lads, but he had to carry most of his own fish in the morning. He was walking along the beach, bowed down with the weight of the catch, when he tripped over a sharp boulder, and it was whispered that someone had put it there on purpose when they saw him coming. Anyhow, he broke his leg badly. Some passersby carried him, howling, to his home and there he's lain ever since. The physician has done what he could, but they say the wound has suppurated and that he will never walk straight again, or command a boat."

She handed me the packet, as one relieved of a great sin, and I sat looking at it for a long time. Then I thanked her, handed it back, and went down to the shore. My father's boat was beached well above the water mark. It looked old and neglected, and I longed to get my hands on it, but it was guarded by a boy, who was putting some touches of pitch to it. I walked on, sometimes throwing aside my tunic and wading into the clear water, rejoicing in its salt coldness after the tepid shallows of Galilee, sometimes flinging myself down on the sand to think deeply.

"Repent—be baptized for the remission of sins—and you shall receive the Holy Spirit." I had no idea whether Jesus, by his Holy Spirit, would really come to me, a Gentile, but the first word *repent*, had been beating in my mind like waves upon the seashore, all the way from Samaria. "You must look at your sin; he will not pour his clean water into a soiled vessel. Repent—repent." I had seen no way to undo the wrong I had done, but now everything was clear. I could repent, if I wanted to; if I was willing to pay the price.

I stayed there for a long time, hating my sin, hating myself and hating, above all, the man who had ruined us. I stayed till the sun made a track of light across the sea and then I rose and ran home. Ione was still up at the big house, but my mother and Illyrica were teasing wool and spinning it into balls. I sat down beside them, and I told them everything; the hate, the yearning for revenge, the burning of the boat and the flight. Then I spoke of the crucifixion, the rumors of the resurrection and the final miracle of Pentecost, but they were not as surprised or horrified as I had imagined they would be. They had suspected all along that my flight was connected with the burning of the boats; they had heard from travelers on the highway about the crucifixion and even rumors of the resurrection, and they had discussed these things among themselves for hours and come to their own conclusions. Only the story of Pentecost was wholly new to them, and they listened spellbound.

"They didn't recognize him as their Messiah, the first time," I insisted. "They crucified him. But now their God is giving them a second chance; he is coming again, in the form of a spirit, to the heart that repents and is baptized for the remission of sins, that's what Peter said. But, in Jerusalem, the message and the promise was only given to the Jews—and yet—" I told them about the woman at Sychar.

My mother did not interrupt me. Only when I had finished speaking, and the room was dark because no one had bothered to light the lamp, did she start to speak.

"That woman was right, Philo. I knew it myself, when I cried in the road between Tyre and Sidon. He is their Messiah, not ours, but he is far, far more. There was another name and he wanted me to find it. 'Help me, Lord,' I cried, and he turned to me immediately. Do demons and storms and sickness and death belong only to Jews? I think he will return to every heart that owns his Lordship and submits to him. Maybe it is there that his kingdom will begin!"

She spoke slowly, groping for words, and I knew that they were the result of many hours of thought. Then Illyrica spoke, and she had always been wise.

"I sometimes think he never really went away," she said quietly. "I think he gave something of himself to those he healed. When I heard that they had crucified him, I wept for his sufferings, but I knew that he was not dead. I thought perhaps he would live on in the cleansed leper, the reclaimed sinner, in the blind man lifting his face to the light. I knew his life could never die. It would live on through death, and perhaps come to perfection somewhere else, far from here. But what you say is better still; tell us again, Philo."

"Repent," I said. "Be baptized for the remission of sins, and you shall receive the gift of the Holy Spirit."

We discussed it at length; to repent was straightforward and even Ione, who had joined the circle just before sunset, was enthusiastic. There was a certain apricot tree in her mistress's garden that she just could not keep away from. To be baptized was harder, for, as far as I knew, only the disciples had authority to baptize. But Joel had said it was a sign, a public confession, and we could tell people what had happened with our lips, as well as with sign language.

"One day," said Illyrica, "I think someone will come and tell us what to do. I think this news will spread to the ends of the earth."

"And if *he* really comes to us," said Ione eagerly, "then *he* will tell us what to do."

It seemed a good idea; none of us older ones had thought of that. But we were all agreed that the first step was to take part of the bride price back to Hiram and to tell him what had happened and, for all I knew, he might well have me beaten and flung into jail. I was very, very frightened but there was no turning back now. Fortunately, there was no difficulty about how much money I should take. He had set his own price. I counted out the double of what he had paid my mother and smiled at the justice of it.

I had good reason to know his house. On stormy nights, when the boats were grounded, Jabin and I had often stalked him home from the tavern, in order to learn his habits and likely routes. It had been a rich man's house in the better quarters of the town when his father was alive, but now, weeds and nettles had sprung up round the door. I knew also that his wife had died in childbirth, not long before, so he was likely be be alone. *He could strangle me*, I thought uneasily, but I knocked on the door all the same.

"Who's there?" growled a savage voice. I drew a long breath and entered.

The room was gloomy and dirty, and the stench

from his wound was terrible. I believe that the boy I had seen in the boat came in twice a day to bring him food and water, but, otherwise, he looked the most wretched, uncared-for creature I had ever seen. He glared at me, and his eyes gleamed with hate and fear.

"What have you come for?" He almost spat the words.

I stood as far away from him as I could and placed the money on the table. "I was one of those who burned your boats," I said abruptly. "I have come to pay for the damage. You fixed the price of a boat with my mother and I have brought the double. I'm sorry and I ask your forgiveness."

"*You—burned—my—boats!* I'll get you in front of the magistrate; I'll have you beaten with rods in the marketplace—" If he could have risen, I think he would have throttled me with his bare hands. I shuddered and turned away. I could not bear either the sight or the smell of him, and all I wanted was to get away from him as far and as fast as possible.

"I'll get even with you," he hissed. "Give me that money."

I tossed it across to him, and he opened the packet greedily. I could see the amazement in his face as the gold pieces tumbled out onto the dirty blanket.

"Did you steal it?" he muttered.

I was angry. I felt he had insulted me. "No, you old fool," I shouted. "If you want to know, it's my sister's bride price. Now, farewell."

"Wait!" He turned his evil face full on me and I shuddered again. "In the name of all the gods, why did you bring it?"

Repent; confess. I supposed this was my chance. "Because I want to have done with sin

187

and start a new, clean life," I said, and then I left him, slamming the door behind me and gulping great draughts of fresh air.

And now, what?

I went back to my favorite haunt, the seashore. After the Galilean summer and the heat of the valleys, I felt I could never have enough of it. I plunged into the sea and lay floating, washing away the corruption of that room, thinking, thinking.

I had done my part, as far as I knew. I had repented, made restitution, confessed. Now it was his turn. If he was coming back to me, now was the moment. I lay there waiting; perhaps I would hear a rushing wind, or praise God in an unknown language, as the disciples had done.

But nothing happened.

"You shall receive the Holy Spirit." It suddenly struck me that perhaps I had not entirely done my part. A gift had to be received. The sun poured itself out on the earth, but the flowers opened their faces to receive the light and the ocean reflected back the colors. Jesus, as far as I knew, had never forced his gifts on anyone. He answered their cry of need, sometimes unspoken. He came when men called.

So for the first time in my life, I prayed to the Supreme God, who had become man. I asked him to come to me.

Nothing happened; at least, nothing that I had expected. But soon, instead of staring at the empty blue sky, a vivid picture came into my mind. I seemed to see a dark room and a man, lying in the gloom, evil and afraid. But this time, I also seemed to see beneath the hate, to the wretchedness and loneliness underneath. It was almost as though I was looking at him with new eyes, with somebody else's eyes.

"Go back," a voice seemed to be saying, "go back now."

I swam in as though in a dream, and dressed. The little booths were beginning to reopen after the noonday siesta. I had a coin in my girdle, and I bought some fruit and a small flask of wine, and when I reached the house I did not knock, I walked straight in, and sat down at the end of his loathsome mattress. I laid the gifts beside him, and he stared at me as though he was seeing a ghost. He was terrified.

"Look," I said, "I'm really sorry about your leg. Is there anything I can do to help you?"

Our eyes held each other for a long moment and I watched the hate and fear drain away, leaving only weariness, misery and despair. His hand plucked at the blanket. "I suppose—" he whispered, and stopped. I knew he was struggling with his pride.

"I suppose—" he tried again. "I suppose you couldn't take on the boat? Find some lads to go with you, and keep the trade going? They say I'll never walk straight again, but you never know."

My father's boat! Just for a moment, I forgot about the man on the bed. I could feel the tarry rope in my hands, the pull of the net. I could hear the slap of black water against the prow and see the dawn breaking over the Tyrian hills. "Of course I will," I said simply, "I'll look over the nets tonight and find some lads. By tomorrow night we'll get her afloat and we'll divide the profits between us all equally."

And suddenly my heart warmed toward this man, and I knew that I was seeing him as Jesus, my God, would have seen him, with eyes of love and compassion and forgiveness.

I knew that we were starting a partnership that was going to last a long time.

I knew too, that the God who had become man, the conqueror of death, demons, sickness and sin, had conquered me. He had come back to me. The kingdom of God was within me.